BELIEVE ME

A Novel by

KEN MCGEE

ISBN: 9798685969347 (paperback)

For Helen Kuenstler, a great teacher
who always pushed me to be better.

Chapter 1

YATES

Every great opportunity in life also contains the potential for ruin. Ryan's father had taught him that maxim, and he thought about it often ever since Robert Yates had retained him as his personal attorney. For a few years the work had been very lucrative as one might expect considering the incredible wealth of his client, but not especially interesting. He drafted the billionaire's pre-nuptial agreement for his future ex-wife, a sullen British model, and saw it successfully hold up in court against the onslaught of a high-priced legal team that did everything to defeat it. After that, he had gained Yates' total trust.

Much of Ryan's other work involved anything considered too sensitive for Yates' team of corporate lawyers. There were some minor lawsuits to be brushed off, one from a slightly schizophrenic cousin back in Missouri, one from an old girlfriend looking for a payday; all were summarily dispatched with little cost other than his own hefty fees. He spent some time scaring various journalists from writing anything that he did not approve. He had grown quite adept at such legal terrorism and extremely wealthy as well. Now, as he slowly drove down the long private road to Yates' compound between Carmel and Pacific Grove, he wondered whether he was in over his head.

"Stop at the white line." That voice which could have been a robot or an actual person with a paucity of human emotion came from what looked like a bush about 30 yards from the main gate. Ryan eased his BMW to a halt where instructed as three men approached him, one carrying an assault rifle. He kept his hands on the steering wheel.

"Roll down your window." The man who seemed in charge of the group looked very seriously at Ryan's car after giving that order. Ryan quickly complied.

"Some new security rules, I see. Everything all right?" His attempt to make small talk went unacknowledged. Usually, this gate was a formality after the team at the bottom of the hill opened his trunk and maneuvered whatever it was underneath his vehicle. The man who stood now with one hip almost touching his rearview mirror reached into his pocket.

"Please look this way, Mr. Monahan." He held up a phone that beeped ever so slightly when Ryan's eyes were in the proper position. In a few seconds, the facial recognition software determined that he was who he was supposed to be. Just then, a small drone buzzed about 20 feet above them and circled a few times before flying off in the distance.

"I have an urgent appointment with Mr. Yates." He tried to assert his authority as the leader still stared at his phone. He kept looking at it as he spoke.

"I am aware of your meeting." The man, who was the type to wear sunglasses inside, might have been the source the robotic voice that had first spoken to him or he might have been a robot. There was a lot of new technology in California. "Please hand me your cell phone. I see that you have no other electronic devices. Is that correct?"

"Yes." Ryan handed over his iPhone without argument wondering whether the little drone had determined the extent of his computer paraphernalia. The man held it with two fingers, as if it might be toxic, before placing it in a small bag. Without a word or any visible signal, the black metal gate swung slowly open. As he drove through the entrance, two unsmiling guards appeared in a jeep and followed him on the drive to the main house while the drone reappeared and followed them all.

Ryan had visited Yates here a few times over the years, feeling always overwhelmed at the almost too perfect scenery, especially as he approached the compound. He had to watch himself on the narrow road for there was much to gawk at. To him it seemed as if the area had been created by a deity that had itself sprung from the mind of Keats with trees and rocks and water and sand that were arranged for perfect design and color. He wondered how many accidents all this beauty had caused.

The main house was flanked by two other stately homes each about five hundred yards away. They had been on this land when Yates gobbled it up ten years earlier, and he had allowed them to remain. One was used as a quarters for his security team, the other was vacant, but was once used as a residence for a bohemian daughter from Yates' first marriage, who had been the fodder for many tabloid stories until Ryan had convinced her that New Zealand would be a wonderful place to live on her trust fund.

The Compound, which was the common way of referring to the Yates mansion proper, had been completed just 18 months earlier as the collaboration between Yates and a Japanese architect, a man fascinated by every geometric shape other than a rectangle. Right and isosceles triangles formed the various sections; octagons, hexagons, and at least one dodecahedron making the home seem both highly logical and disturbing, much like its owner. When he pulled up in front, the guards turned around, but the drone circled overhead.

"Good morning, Mr. Monahan." Milla van Dine, who had obviously been informed of his impending arrival, stood outside of the opaque glass doors of the entrance flanked by two imposing English Mastiffs who stared intensely at him as he got out of the car. He carried the little folder, the purpose of his visit, above his shoulders in case one of the dogs might decide to chew it up. Milla was wearing a long white spa robe and had let her long blonde hair down for the first time in Ryan's presence, locks that reached the middle of her back and appeared to be the healthiest that he had ever seen. That made sense because one of her many duties was to be the "guardian," as she described it, of the well-being and physical perfection of Robert Yates.

"Are you going to frisk me before I come in or are those dogs trained to detect any bad intentions on the part of visitors?" She smiled showing her perfect incisors. Ryan was a few years older than Milla, but she appeared unaffected by any experience of the world he might possess. When he first met her, he had briefly considered the possibility of asking her to dinner, but he had found her too daunting for him to approach. Living in Los Angeles for ten years, he had been with some incredibly beautiful women; none had exuded confidence like Milla.

"Yes, there are some increased security concerns just now, and I apologize for any inconvenience." She kept her hands at her side, greeting him only with the slightest bow of her head. Ryan made the same bow keeping his eyes on those dogs. Milla pressed her phone, and the huge glass doors oozed open to reveal the marble flooring of the foyer that appeared to have been very recently polished.

"Is this the butler's day off?" Rolf, a distinguished looking Danish gentleman, usually met him at the door without dogs. Milla stepped out of her sandals, and he kicked off his loafers.

"You are such a big deal that Mr. Yates wants to be completely alone with you for this meeting. There's just me and a few people in the kitchen in case you get hungry." She took Ryan's arm as she said this.

"Mr. Yates likes his privacy." He wondered how much she knew about what he had brought with him. Milla seemed to be indispensable within the compound. She supervised the staff to include security; she was Yates' yoga instructor trainer, dietician, decorator and, as he learned on his last trip, masseuse. Other duties were possible and even suspected by the ex-wife though she could never prove anything. In the judge's chamber during the divorce proceedings, she referred to Milla as her husband's "bhakti whore."

"Heel!" Milla said this in a low voice, and the dogs froze in their tracks just as the four of them were about to enter the wing of the house where Robert Yates spent most of his time on the earth. They passed a gym as large as a Gold's with an indoor pool that connected to another outside, a cigar room with a huge cedar humidor, a video game room that seemed largely unused, and two master bedrooms that Ryan had never seen. There was also, what someone might call a family room if a family consisted of fifty people. That was where they found Yates sitting in his ten-person whirlpool tub in one corner grinning the way the 12th richest man in the world is supposed to grin all the time.

"Ah, young Ryan. Perfectly punctual as always." He stood up and grabbed a towel as he ascended from the tub, undismayed by his brief nudity. He was in his late sixties, but had the body of a man in his forties in great shape with an actual six-pack abdomen. Milla had been doing her job very well.

"Will we be working in your office, sir?" Yates seldom wanted small talk when there was business to conduct. There was also a formal office in the wing that was an exact copy of a drawing room in Versailles, complete with a ceiling mural. Ryan loved working in that room and thought it might make the day's discussion more enjoyable.

"No, let's just do it in here. The view is much more conducive to clear thinking and creativity." The view was spectacular as the solid twenty-foot wall of windows revealed the blue sky and even bluer ocean. To the left was the unnatural green of Pebble Beach. Ryan waited for Yates to put on a robe identical to Milla's and point to the couch before he took a seat. Yates could be informal and imperious at the same time. Milla went behind the oak bar to fix them both a Pellegrino with lime before getting something thick and moss green for herself.

"So, have you read this thing, this mystery document that someone wants to use to blackmail me?" Yates pointed to the document that now sat on Ryan's lap. He had not dried his feet well, and he left tiny puddles on the wood floor as he paced back and forth swigging his drink as if he had just stepped out of the desert.

"Yes, I have." He looked pointedly at Milla wondering when the boss would dismiss her to allow them to begin the discussion in earnest. Yates noticed his hesitation and laughed.

"Milla knows all about it, young man." He motioned for her to sit on the couch across from Ryan. "Of course, she doesn't know exactly what this is because even I don't know." He took another drink. "So what is it?"

"It appears to be a sort of brief memoir by someone named Ben Ford about things that he claims happened to him in Saint Louis." Ryan was perversely taking some enjoyment from briefly knowing more than Yates about anything important.

"Never heard of him."

"You wouldn't. He is an absolute nobody even by Missouri standards." He took a drink of his own to continue the suspense. "But he may have been involved recently with Anna Dare." He wanted to give Yates another chance to send Milla away. "That is, if the document is not a fake."

"Why would anyone care what this nonentity has to say?" He took a seat next to Milla on the couch, not touching, but close. "Who knew enough about you to send it to you with instructions to make sure that I am aware of it?"

"I don't know for certain, but the hand written note accompanying it was signed by Ms. Dare or someone claiming to be her. I have been unable to verify the signature." Yates turned his head and ordered the room to be two degrees cooler and the air conditioner made a small noise as it commenced.

"And what did that note say again, exactly?" Ryan produced the slip of paper and read aloud.

"Please make Robert Yates aware of this little story which he may find interesting. Further instructions will follow. Thank you." The signature was elaborate and precise with the capital "a" a sharp arch with a bow joining the two legs. The rest of the cursive seemed to be the work of someone who had received top grades in penmanship forty years ago when such things mattered.

"Instructions? Sounds like a threat to me, doesn't it to you?" Yates said this to Milla who did not react. For a moment, Ryan wondered just how much Yates knew about any of this. He had a trick of making others feel smarter than he was about some subject, a feeling that made them over-confident and weaker. It was possible that Yates had arranged to have him receive this document personally in order to give himself some deniability. He again felt the vague threat he had been experiencing since the courier had left his office yesterday.

"It could just be seen as the ravings of a disturbed young man, but in the wrong hands it could be seen as something very damaging, very damaging to you, sir." Ryan stopped there to indicate once again that they should discuss the situation in private. He was convinced by the look on Yates' face that, although he was not concerned, he was ignorant of the contents of the document. That and having Milla regard him with a look that resembled intense interest made him feel quite proud of himself.

"So many disturbed people are associated with Anna Dare. It's disturbing." Yates waited for Ryan to acknowledge his witticism with a wry smile before continuing. "How did he manage to write so much about what you said were recent events?" He was only slightly annoyed, but enough for Ryan to be wary.

"According to him, he was sequestered in some house in the wilds of Missouri. He had nothing else to do for thirty days, but record this story." He tapped the document. "Ford says that Anna Dare paid him a million dollars to do it." Yates gave Milla a look that suggested he was surprised what people would do for a mere million dollars.

"And why would Anna Dare do such a thing with her hard-earned money?" He was curious, but also dismissive of the concept.

"It is not clear to me just from reading this why she did it or even, of course, if she did it at all." He thought a second. "The thing is, this Ford appears to be easily influenced by financial incentives." He felt that he should make sure that Yates retained his feeling of invincibility, the feeling that ridiculously rich men enjoyed above all others. Knowing that a potential adversary had a price would make him confident that all would be well. Maybe it would turn out well for everyone involved with this mess. Ryan was not sure.

"Dear, dear Anna Dare. It has been more than a month since anyone has heard a peep out of her. Even my brother seems unable to reach her which is unusual even if she is on some sort of spiritual retreat or whatever she said." He closed his eyes for a moment as if he might be about to express some regret about Anna. During the silence, Milla crossed her legs causing the robe to expose one perfect calf. "Has she been hiding out with this Ben Ford?"

"He says that he has been completely alone if you choose to believe him."

"Do you have a reason to doubt his veracity?" Milla said this, and Ryan had to control the temptation to raise an eyebrow at her question. Since Yates did not appear to consider her impertinent, Ryan accepted that she was an active participant in the discussion. The bare foot of her crossed leg did not twitch even a little with nervousness, and he answered her directly.

"I question every story, unless there are eyewitnesses who can verify its veracity, and even then things are questionable. Or can be questioned in a court of law." Ryan turned to Yates, his client paying his hefty fee, as he delivered the last line.

"That's my Roy Cohn. There's always a way to discredit anyone who says something unfavorable about me." He said that to Milla whose look must have made him consider her question. "But is this guy telling the truth?"

"You will have to be the judge of that after you read it." He did not appreciate the Roy Cohn reference, but he let it slide. Working for this client had induced him to let many things slide. Yates stood up and took some time opening a bottle of a 2015 Chateau Lafite Rothschild (he mentioned what it was) and pouring three glasses with a flourish. He handed Milla hers, but Ryan went to the bar to claim his own. It tasted like gold.

"Well, It looks like there is nothing else to do, but for you to read it to us. If Anna Dare sent this, she must want something, and we will have to figure out what that thing is together. So it's story time." There it was. The man had fully reasserted his authority and his potential mastery of any situation, and Ryan quickly accepted that scenario. It was comfortable for both of them, and for Milla who continued to swirl and sniff her wine without taking a sip as if it might be toxic. Without hesitation or complaint, he carefully set down his glass, picked up the document, and started to read.

Chapter 2

BEN FORD

By the time anyone reads this, I will probably be dead. I, Ben Ford, am certainly not of sound mind considering recent events, but I have done what was asked of me. I will freely admit that I did it initially for financial gain, but something else seems to have happened to me during this process. It could simply be the result of absolute isolation; there is no internet or television in this house, which rendered me truly alone for the first time in my life. Constant thoughts of being discovered by people who would enjoy doing me harm probably contributed to my mental state. Maybe all of those effects were calculated. I don't know.

I am confused about exactly why I am doing this or why I need to be cut off from the world to do it, but that was what Anna wanted. I have no idea whether she will fulfill her part of the bargain. In fact, I have no way of knowing whether any of the people important to this story are still alive. I hope I am wrong about that, but certain events have made me fully aware of the cheap price that many people place on human life.

This small house is in Jackson County, Missouri, which some people believe will be the sight of the Second Coming. I assume that was just a coincidence in the choice of this sight, but you never know. There is so much that I do not know about the world, but I am bound to tell my story, no matter what happens after.

I did my best to be honest in writing this, leaving nothing out, even though it makes me seem less than heroic. Upon rereading it, I imagine that many would judge me cowardly, especially considering the quickness of my decision to hide out here instead of taking some action, but that is what occurred. I freely admit that after my last week in Saint Louis I needed some sense of safety, and I needed even more time to think about everything that has happened and may happen next. My life has changed forever. Going from nothing to a sudden abundance is not as wonderful as you may think. When you have nothing, the world leaves you mostly alone; the minute you have something, you have to wonder how soon it will be taken away.

For what it is worth, here is my story.

Chapter 3

BEN FORD

I was wide-awake, and none of the usual procedures to make me sleep were working. The steady rotation of TV channels between a documentary about the Fukishima disaster and an Australian Rules football game made me more jumpy than drowsy. There were pills in my backpack, of course, but I was not certain of their strength having obtained them outside of the advice of medical professionals. I needed to be up early with no trace of a drug hangover clouding my brain. I turned off the TV and stared for a while at the beige ceiling of the Drury Inn. I went through the fifty states and capitals, both alphabetically and from east to west with no noticeable effect.

I was back in Saint Louis for the first time in over two years. Actually, I was in Saint Charles, that old/new city just across the Missouri river and a short drive from where I needed to be. In my head, I made the same geographical adjustment that everyone in the area tends to make, telling people they meet in Hawaii that they are from Saint Louis when they live ten miles outside the city limits. The old town's history easily eradicates their little suburb from the conversation. For the first ten years of my life, until the death of my parents, I had lived in Saint

Charles, before spending the rest of my youth in Chesterfield, Missouri, another city no one claimed to be from when talking to strangers from New York.

When my cell phone rang, I didn't have to look at the number to know who it was although I was surprised that my grandmother was calling after 10. I had left a message while driving that morning to tell them the news and where I was. Her voice sounded tired.

"Benny. How are you? Are you still driving?"

"No, Grandma. I am at a motel all safe and sound." She never wanted me to talk while I was driving. "I am surprised that you are calling me so late. It's after eleven in Florida."

"I stay up all hours now. Something about this new medication. Anyway, I only just heard your message since our phone no longer beeps any more unless you pick it up." She paused. "I am so sorry to hear about your Uncle Al."

"I know. It was a shock."

"Was it a heart attack?"

"The lawyer I spoke to said they thought it was a stroke." She sighed.

"Those happen when you get old. That's for sure." She was letting me know that I had not called her in many months, and she and my grandfather were older than Uncle Al.

"I know."

"I'll say a prayer for him. And I will say one for you."

"Thanks."

"Benny, you said something in your message about a reading of your uncle's will."

"Yes, that's tomorrow morning."

"And there's no service or any place we can send flowers?" She sounded upset about that.

"No. It has all been taken care of."

"I see." She was disapproving of something, probably everything in the situation. "Well, if you do inherit some money, please promise me you will speak to your grandfather before you do anything." I could tell that she wanted to add "foolish" to the end of that sentence. I didn't blame her, considering my past irresponsibility with money and Life in general.

"I will do that, but I need to get some sleep now. You should too."

"Yes. You must be exhausted from that long drive all the way from Alabama. Are you still living there?" She knew exactly how to make me feel like a crappy grandson while maintaining an air of grandmotherly concern.

"I sort of live there." I could see she didn't want to ask for details, and I didn't want to offer any. Neither of us would have liked the part about me following some woman down there after dating her for less than two months, then breaking up with her and not having the energy to leave.

"Well, remember what I said. Your grandpa plays golf every morning, but he is mostly free the rest of the day. He would love to hear from you and give you any advice you need." When I didn't reply immediately to that, we both said an awkward, "love you" and hung up leaving me with even more anxiety.

My parents died when I was six, both killed when the motorcycle they were riding was t-boned by an uninsured, drunk driver in a large pickup truck. My mother's parents raised me. They were good to me in most of the ways to judge such things, but I came to understand that they had never approved of my father and of my mother for marrying him. Their death seemed to justify that opinion. I suppose they could not help to see something of my father's unacceptable character in me, and many of my failures, especially dropping out of college, had justified that opinion as well.

Those grandparents also had a zip code snobbery about Saint Charles, maintaining that it only existed to receive the White Flight from North Saint Louis County. That may have been true for some, but my parents had moved there when I was two simply to get an affordable condominium along Highway 94. Of course, I had no idea what the place was like now. I had arrived late driving up from Alabama and had not seen much of the city. The motel was in a sort of village setting with restaurants, shops, and even a movie theater. After checking in I had driven under Highway 70 to a Denny's to eat, a place where no one would find it strange that I was in a booth alone.

I got up and looked at those pills wondering whether the coffee at Denny's had truly been decaf. I did not like the way my mind was bouncing all over the place. For one thing, the meeting early the next morning was in Ferguson, Missouri, that infamous little town in Saint Louis County that became synonymous with many things concerning crime, police brutality, protests, and all of the racial divides that made people pause before stopping there for gas. Even though I had been in that town many times, I felt a little nervous about the trip.

Secondly, my life was at an ugly dead end. I was 28, a college dropout working at a terrible, mindless job as a furniture mover because I had no interest in taking any steps to improve my circumstances. I was an absolute loser in the game of life, and in the 21st century, it is almost impossible to change your course once things go wrong. The future looked like a dark hole opening up in front of me waiting to swallow me whole.

The overriding cause for my anxiety was the reason for my sudden visit. The next morning I would be attending a reading of my great Uncle Al's will in his hometown of Ferguson. He had died suddenly of a stroke two weeks earlier although I only heard about it when the notice of the will reading reached me in Alabama. It might not have reached me at all, but the woman I had been living with until six months ago, the one I had followed to Alabama, thought that a letter from a lawyer might be important and called me. I felt a terrible guilt not only from not staying in touch with my uncle, who had been very kind to me over the years, but also because I was feeling a sick sense of anticipation at being about to receive money from his estate the next day. Even though I needed money, I could not help thinking what a terrible person I was to feel lucky at such a time.

I turned the TV back on and scrolled through the channels again giving each a few seconds to draw my interest, but nothing did. There must have been a big forest fire somewhere as the same pictures of an uncontrolled blaze appeared on three stations. The Aussies still played their indecipherable game. There was pay-per-view porn with titles that made me queasy at the clever attempts to manipulate my solitary male desire like some lab rat. I listened to a music channel for a while amazed that a song by the Shop Boyz, released the year I started driving, sounded so dated.

I turned the set off again and decided to read the thing I had been avoiding. When Lisa, that former girlfriend, had called me about the lawyer's announcement, she had also given me a letter from a few weeks earlier that she had not thought urgent enough to contact me about, the address being handwritten. It was from my Uncle Al causing me to experience the twin shock of learning of his death, only to receive a final communication from beyond the grave. Not that the letter said much of anything. He had just been going through some old papers and found something that my mother had written years ago which he thought might be interesting to me. He asked also that I call him sometime just to talk.

The paper that he enclosed was in the side pocket of my backpack, my only luggage. I fished it out and set it next to me on the bed. It was a yellowed page of notebook paper covered with my mother's precise, yet archly skewed cursive. When I first read it in the car outside of Lisa's apartment, I knew exactly what it was. My mother occasionally toyed with the idea, when she wasn't teaching kindergarten, of writing a children's book. It had a title called *Sweet Dreams* or something. She told me once that it would just be a collection of the stories she told me at bedtime to help me go to sleep, and the handwritten paper was a fragment of one of those, something I had last heard almost 20 years ago when she was still on this earth. I read it again in that empty hotel room.

Four miracles are occurring simultaneously as your sleepy eyes read this.

First, the giant world you live on, this immobile, most solid thing is shifting its great weight back toward the sun to find the light of tomorrow. It turns this way perfectly every night and has for billions of nights without fail. (The bright toy ball of the sun, by the way, could swallow a million Earths and have room for more.)

Second, this same orb (remember learning that word?) flies at a terrible speed on a long journey around that same sun even as it spins. It follows some complicated laws to do this which you will learn about soon enough, though it will continue whether you learn them or not.

Third, as you glide effortlessly through space, many tiny things, things much too small to see, work away inside you, keeping you well and strong, pushing your bones to stretch and grow in a process that is magic itself. Again, you never need to think about it; it just happens.

Fourth, is the simple fact of you, my beautiful boy. It is a miracle that you exist and that my words can flow from this page into your sleepy brain, and, in a flash of light, you can see the world that I am thinking of, and you can feel my love in those words forever.

Consider for a long moment these miracles. They will go on no matter where you are.

I read it twice, closed my eyes, and went to sleep.

Chapter 4

BEN FORD

Driving to Ferguson from Saint Charles is easy. It is just a short trip down Highway 70 after crossing the Missouri River by way of the comically generic bridge that has a name that no one ever uses, so mundane is its design. Jobs were still mostly east of the river so the traffic was heavy, but swift. At breakfast that morning at a modern place right beside the hotel called First Watch (quinoa pancakes) the hostess was a young black woman who seated me next to an interracial couple trying to get their infant daughter to eat scrambled eggs. Maybe things were changing.

I passed the airport realizing that it would have been smarter to stay in one of the massive hotels that surround it. Oh, I had gotten a good rate in Saint Charles, but I really think I had some foolish notion about wanting to stay in the same zip code where I had lived when my parents were still alive. Once upon a time, I would have stayed in Chesterfield, but my grandparents had moved three years earlier to Florida, and my old friendships from high school and college had lapsed after I became such a loser. All my friends had good jobs, wives who did yoga, cute designer pets or cuter kids, and everyone took great vacations to cool places. To avoid knowing about such things, I had quit Facebook and all social media, even trashing my email account in a fit of dejection after my breakup with Lisa. For my generation, such a decision is a kind of suicide since your existence, once unverifiable, ceases.

Although I was pretty sure of the first part of the route, I had given Siri the address and her calm voice confirmed that I get off the highway at Florissant Road to enter Ferguson. I was nervous, not having been there since the riots, but there was really nothing threatening about the place. It appeared like any poor city in America with some houses needing work, but none looking condemned. Although I didn't see any abandoned cars on the side of the road, there were very few fast food chains, those beacons of American comfort and security that make most cities look the same. An older woman sitting on a bus stop bench smiled as if she were just happy to be alive that day.

Siri directed me to make a few turns until announcing my arrival in front of an old brick building that seemed to have been partially refurbished with new windows, but still sported a very shabby roof. A small sign suspended above the door was a wooden hand with a downward pointing finger that said "lawyer" on it. There was no name of the firm written anywhere I could see. Not wanting to question Siri, I parked in a weedy lot behind the place between a new Lexus and a very old Taurus with chipped paint. It almost made my crummy Civic look respectable.

The small waiting room consisted of six yellow plastic chairs with a receptionist desk at the far end from the door. The only person sitting on one of the plastic chairs was an old man wearing a Cardinal's hat reading the paper. He did not look up when I entered. The receptionist, who seemed to be a recent high school graduate, did acknowledge me with a smile. When I told her my name, she nodded as if expecting me. Offering me some coffee in a paper cup, she immediately hurried through the door to the lawyer's office. I sat down across from the old man, who was now looking over his glasses at me.

"So you're Ben?" I nodded. "I'm Joe Bailey. I worked at the post office with your uncle for 40 years and had breakfast with him almost every day since we retired." I nodded again without knowing what my reaction was supposed to be to that information. Just then, the office door swung open, and a huge black man sporting a red tie and a short-sleeved white shirt entered the waiting room.

"Good morning, gentlemen! Thank you for your punctuality." He pumped both of our hands introducing himself as Richard Jeffers, the executor of Uncle Al's estate. In a moment we were in his office, a room covered in the thinnest brown paneling sold at Lowe's. The only decorations on the walls were a couple of framed diplomas and a photograph of Martin Luther King making a speech. There was something slightly sturdier than a card table perpendicular to the large mahogany desk. We all took seats around it after Jeffers handed us copies of the will. I was wondering where we would have put any other heirs. The lawyer spoke, deepening his tone as if he were recording the event.

"This is the Last Will and Testament of Albert James Ford, which I, as his appointed executor, do faithfully execute on this day…" He went on for a while with a lot of very formal language as I stared at the slim document in front of me. I was a little surprised that he did not offer any condolences for our loss, but he seemed oddly excited to get on with the reading. He went quickly through the first page, but Bailey, who flipped to the end, stopped him.

"So this is dated just two months ago on March sixth?" The lawyer smiled broadly, but seemed annoyed by the interruption.

"Yes, sir. He came in here very anxious to have these papers drawn up. Very anxious." He turned to look at me. "I don't know if your uncle had a premonition that he was about to be called, but he seemed most determined to have this completed as soon as possible." He took a deep breath and continued eager again to get to something we had not seen.

And there it was. Bailey got $40,000 dollars along with a jokey stipulation that he had to buy a new car with the money (not enforceable, Jeffers pointed out). I, on the other hand, received more than I had ever dreamed, more than I could have imagined my uncle accumulating under any circumstances. In my head, I calculated that it was 11 years of my total current income, even with good tips, from humping people's absurdly heavy sleeper sofas up narrow stairs. This was not counting whatever I could get for his house, which was mine as well. Sitting in this little office in Ferguson, I had suddenly become, for me, stupidly rich. Jeffers could see my shock.

"It is amazing what some men with clever investment strategies manage to save over the course of their lives." I am ashamed to say it, but it was very difficult for me to control my emotions just then; it was difficult to just sit there and not jump up and scream with joy. I was wondering whether Jeffers had ever seen an inheritance of this size in Ferguson. Maybe that's why he had been anxious about the reading.

"Amazing." Bailey said this in a sarcastic tone, and I supposed that he was pissed about getting so little compared to the ne'er do well millennial nephew, who had not been to see his uncle in years. I know how these old guys think, and, to some extent, I agreed with him. Still, my guilt was being crowded out of my mind as the calculations began translating the money into cars and trips and things I had stopped thinking about.

"Now these accounts at the bank are POD, so they will be very easy to claim. I have written down the account numbers and the manager's name for you." He handed me a separate sheet of paper.

"POD?" I had not heard the term.

"Payable on Death. The accounts just become yours with no action required by the court or anyone." The lawyer seemed very happy for me, and he was right to be. Before the meeting, I had about $700 in the bank and $70 in my wallet and no other assets outside of my old car. He read the rest of the will, but I didn't hear much of it. There was some woman named Florence who got something or other; she turned out to be in a nursing home and was unable to make the trip to his office today. I didn't care.

Eventually, the meeting ended. Bailey got his check while I was handed the keys to my uncle's house and car (the fairly new Camry was also a part of my haul). I walked past the receptionist in a daze still trying not to smile. Outside, the old man and I made our way to the back of the building in silence. Just as I reached my car, he decided to speak.

"You want to get a coffee or something with me? There's a place just a few blocks up from here." When I didn't immediately respond, he began slapping the check he was holding against the palm of his other hand. "There's some things you need to know about."

"Sure." I really didn't want to go, but I was still experiencing some guilt about neglecting my uncle that made me feel obligated to listen to whatever this old guy wanted to say, as if I could atone for past sins by spending time with some random senior citizen. I'm not sure I even understood that at the time, but I got in my car and followed him a mile or so to a place called Violet's Café.

It was a well-lit place and uncrowded at near ten in the morning with booths and tables that looked new and recently cleaned. A young man sweeping the floor as we entered seemed to be dancing with his broom to the old Motown sounds coming out of the ceiling speakers. The walls were decorated with various paintings that seemed to be amateur but fun. One of them featured King Kong hanging calmly by one hand from the Arch as Godzilla crossed the Mississippi behind him.

"Mr. Bailey! We have missed you. You been goin' up to McDonald's for those sausage biscuits and fake potatoes?" A black woman about 50 danced her way toward us also affected by the song that was playing.

"No, ma'am. I've been out of town visiting my daughter until just the other day. What kind of pie is good today?"

"They all good, but you got a weak spot for the cherry, don't you?"

He seemed pretty excited about the pie, and we took a seat in one of the far booths. The woman, who turned out to be Violet, brought us coffee and the biggest piece of cherry pie I had ever seen in a restaurant. When Bailey told her who I was, she gave me a big hug and told me what a great guy my uncle was. She seemed to mean it, and I saw a little tear in her eye as she was leaving us. Bailey savored each bite of his pie and was several in before he spoke.

"So what did this lawyer tell you about your uncle's death?"

"Just that he had a stroke in the parking lot of a Schnuck's." Schnuck's was the St. Louis grocery chain whose name visitors found hilarious. It felt comfortable, after being away for a few years, to say it again.

"That's how I heard it." He slowly chewed some more pie. "The thing is, by the time I heard about it, this lawyer I never heard your uncle mention even one time, had already had his body cremated and buried. Does that strike you as unusual?" Even though I was glad he wasn't giving me a hard time about not appreciating my uncle, I didn't like where he was going with this. I said something about such things probably happening all the time when people don't have much family in the area.

"I suppose that's true enough, but your uncle and I had breakfast every morning, usually right here. Don't you find it unusual that he had a fatal stroke, the first one I'd ever heard about him having, at the same time I am out of town for my one trip a year to see my daughter in Seattle?" He was agitated, but it did not slow down his steady assault on the pie. I was thinking about saying something about Uncle Al's eating habits that might have contributed to a stroke, but thought better of it.

"I'm sure they called the paramedics and the cops, whoever found him. If he would have been attacked in some way, they would have noticed it." I was trying to calm him down as well as I could.

"The police don't look too close at 76 year old men dropping dead with all the other things they have to worry about unless they have a knife sticking out of their back." He leaned forward and lowered the volume of his voice. "You know about this Anna Dare?"

"I've heard about her, sure. She's the woman who won the big Powerball and moved to Ferguson." I had seen a 60 Minutes report on her, but I had been playing Faster than Light on my phone most of the time, so the details were sketchy.

"She won the Powerball twice, two of the biggest jackpots ever, and then she announced that God had given her the numbers. Then she wrote a book that is supposed to be some kind of new Gospel, and people, not just around here, but all over the world, have started treating her like a prophet or some such thing." Violet had come up behind him with the coffee pot as he spoke those words.

"You all talkin' about Miss Anna? Guess what? She came in here just last week for breakfast. I recognized her from the TV, but I didn't say nothing. It was just her and some dude who didn't look like no bodyguard for sure. Can you believe that? Woman with all that money out with no protection at all."

"Yes, I've heard she shows up all over town." Bailey was being polite, but I could tell he was wanting her to leave us alone.

"Maybe she do, but she was right over there eatin' my pancakes as big as you please. Know what she did? She asked me about those pictures on the wall that did have little price tags on them. I told her they all done by kids up at the high school, and she bought every single one of them right then and there. She didn't make no show out of it, just wrote me a check and said she'd be sending somebody over to pick them up. Them kids was thrilled." She held up her hand not holding the coffee pot. "So all I say is hallelujah and praise be to her!" Bailey sighed after she walked away.

"This Dare woman seems to have that effect on many people. That much money is something around here." He woofed down the last morsel of pie. "The interesting thing is your uncle got tied up with her in some way. I don't know exactly how. He told me that he knew her from the old days in Ferguson."

"She is from here?" I really wanted to go, but I was surprised at that.

"Yes, a McCluer High School girl back in the 60s when things were still golden around here.

"Interesting." I said that, but was still not truly interested.

"Anyway, I was up on Calverton Road about a month ago, and I swore I saw Al being let through the gate she had put up at that big old house she bought. When I asked him about it, he clammed up in a way I'd never seen before."

"Maybe he did know her, but was embarrassed about going to see her now that she was rich. I guess we'll never know." He could tell I was losing interest.

"I just think it's funny that your uncle died, and the only people who might have asked questions were bought off with money that there is no way he ever saved from working at the Post office." When I didn't react, he held up his hand. "I just felt I needed to tell you that, son. I'm too old to do much with the information."

I thanked him as best I could, considering I thought him to be another crazy old guy with conspiracy theories about anything that happened. There was always something hidden, some sinister plot. I went up front to pay the check handing Dora the credit card that I now had no qualms about using since the least I could do was buy the old man some pie with some of my new money.

"You gonna go by and look at Miss Anna's house while you in town? It's just a few blocks over. Quite a site for Ferguson."

"I might just do that." I am a terrible liar, and she could tell I had no intention of doing it.

"I read her book. Everybody should." She gripped my hand as I was handing back the pen I'd used to sign the receipt. "You know, they's a lot of love here in Ferguson. But it's the love you got for your man or your woman or your family. Lots of that all over. What we ain't got much of anywhere is the love for them that ain't yours, who you might only see one time. That's the love Jesus talked about, and Miss Anna sayin' the same thing." She squeezed my hand hard. I nodded.

I took my leave of her and Bailey without much further discussion. I drove back up to Florissant Road to get to my uncle's side street while feeling for the house key in my pocket. Just before the turn I saw a billboard that featured a pair of unusually large blue eyes, the woman's face they belonged to faded and unrecognizable. The eyes were haunting, but exuded a kindness that was calming. On the bottom of the billboard small red letters spelled out "Anna Lives Here" and nothing else.

Chapter 5

YATES

"Jesus, what a loser this guy is." He went to the bar, opened a Red Bull, drank some, and poured a shot of vodka into the can. Milla stood up and pulled her hair on top of her head with a clip as if she were alone in the room. Ryan waited for Yates to continue which he did. "He didn't even know who Anna Dare was a few weeks ago? How is that possible? Doesn't Alabama have Wi-Fi?" Milla looked at his can of Red Bull as if she knew it contained vodka and was not happy.

"He seemed to have given up on the world. People do that, and then they don't care what happens in it." She slowly bent from the waist until her palms were flat on the floor, holding them there for a full minute before straightening up.

"He's a complete moron, and I have no idea why his sad story is worth my time." At that moment, Ryan thought the meeting was about to end abruptly and decided that he should make a suggestion as a responsible attorney.

"I have marked some particular parts that I think you should look at, sir. They might shed some light on the motivation behind whoever sent this." Once again, he was just trying to protect his client. Milla shook her head, her face still flushed from being so long toward the floor.

"I think we should hear the whole story and not just selected passages." Ryan took a sip of wine and looked to Yates, waiting for him to take charge.

"I suppose that there might be some value added in hearing every bit of his story. It might give us an understanding of how these people live in the middle of the country, all full of pie and opioids with no real comprehension of what is going on in the real world." He sat back down on the sofa and Milla sat down a little closer to him than before.

"There is quite a bit left, sir." When Ryan was considering the offer to become the personal attorney for Robert Yates, he consulted with his old law professor at Stanford. The man had been adamant about his refusing the position. Not only would it consume all of his time, rendering the rest of his practice insignificant, but it would also be very stressful in that the temptation to please such a powerful man could lead to a blurring of ethical lines that would be his undoing. "You will be there to insulate him from harm, and when the heat is on, the insulation melts first."

"It's the easiest few hours you will ever get to bill me for. Look at it that way." His good humor and sense of authority were back in full view. "Besides, I have some curiosity about this little dope and what made Anna care about him at all that requires some satisfaction." Milla tucked her legs up underneath her on the couch brushing Yates' knee with her toe in the motion.

"Shall we continue, then?" Yates just nodded.

Chapter 6

BEN FORD

On the way to my uncle's house, I decided that Bailey was just a poor old guy whose grief at losing his only companion needed a sort of fantastic explanation for him to bear it. He had mentioned that his wife had died three years earlier so now he was truly alone in the world. Although I had been alone for some months since moving out of Lisa's place, for an old man there would seem to be no hope left. I also had no curiosity about where my uncle's money had come from. At that point my mind was still buzzing with the possibilities of the ways I might spend it drowning out most other thoughts.

My uncle's block was quiet as you might expect on a weekday morning; people with jobs or school were already gone, the rest sleeping in. The neighborhood looked shabby only in parts with just a few houses needing paint or gutter repairs. His house (my house, but I could not quite think that way yet) was in great shape with new siding and a crack free driveway. I felt a flash of nervousness going up to the empty place alone. Some of this had to do with entering the house of a dead person and some was about being a white man on his own in Ferguson. I looked around the neighborhood as I mounted the steps to the front door watching for any sudden movements.

When I turned the key and opened the door, all hell broke loose. A high pitched alarm went off immediately making me cover my ears and freeze there on the stone porch, not wanting to enter, but afraid to just leave. After a full minute I went back to my car wondering whether Jeffers would know how to turn it off before the Ferguson cops arrived looking for a burglar. Some neighbors stuck their heads out of front doors. I held up my hands in the universal sign of helplessness, but I doubt they were looking at me. As I fumbled around trying to find Jeffers' business card, I saw a young woman running toward the house with the speed and form of a middle distance runner. She gave me only a brief look as she went past my car, going up the short steps in two bounds and entering the house through the still open door.

Instantly the alarm ceased. By the time I got out of the car the runner was standing just outside the front door with her hands on her hips breathing hard, but not winded. She was wearing an old Mizzou t-shirt and sweat pants with her hair pulled into a kind of sideways ponytail. Because this was Ferguson, I assumed she was African-American, but as I got closer, I could tell that her ethnicity was complicated. Although I hate it when men give women a numerical rating, she was beautiful enough to earn a very high number even in her casual state. From my perspective at the bottom of the steps I could not tell whether she was taller than me, but it was close. She held out her hand to stop me on the third step.

"You got business here?" She was looking straight into my eyes without smiling. Suddenly, I realized that I might be about to have a confrontation with a local woman (she seemed slightly older than I was) from Ferguson unless I weighed my words carefully.

"This is my uncle's house." I spoke slowly staying right where I was on the steps. "He just passed away, and I inherited it." She did smile now with all of her teeth.

"You, Ben?" She moved back a few steps so that my ascent was no longer blocked.

"Yes, I'm Ben Ford." I was even with her now on the porch and a comfortable inch taller though she was wearing running shoes. "I don't remember Uncle Al having an alarm."

"I can see that." I had the distinct impression that she was studying me in a way I had not been looked at in some time and certainly not by a woman who, now that I was only a foot away from her, was well out of my league physically. She held out her hand. "I'm Nicole Rice. Nicki." We exchanged a formal handshake. I tried not to think anything about her touch, but I did. She was really a beauty.

"I guess the cops will be here soon. Maybe you can vouch for me." Although I thought about just touching her on the shoulder in a friendly way, I didn't. She laughed.

"Nah, they won't be coming. Ain't nobody round here called them. Old Al never hooked it up to contact anybody, just scare the crap out of people trying to kick open his door."

"You knew my uncle pretty well, then?" This came out awkwardly because it was hard to look at her without staring. I couldn't tell if she knew the effect she was having; some women didn't.

"Yeah, he was a great old guy. I cleaned house for him." She stretched her arms above her head in a nonchalant way. "I got my own cleaning business, and he was one of my first customers. That's why I know the alarm code."

"Lucky for me you were around." I was flirting now, and she seemed receptive to it. I knew some women who cleaned houses for a living, and they always had a sense of the wealth of their clients from this Schwab notice left on the desk to that bank statement on the nightstand. This

Nicki knew something about what I had inherited, and it interested her. That was what I thought.

"I stay just across the street." She gestured with her hand toward an older house with a weedy lawn. "You thinkin' about moving in here? Bein' my neighbor?"

"I don't know. I just found out that it was my house this morning." I was pretty sure that I would be selling it, but I did not want to seem as if the idea of moving to Ferguson was out of the question since it was her neighborhood. "I just got in town last night from out of state, and I'm staying at a hotel in St. Charles." That was a dumb thing to say, but she didn't react.

"It's a very nice house." I was wondering about that statement when she handed me a business card advertising Clean as a Whistle Maid Service with her name and phone number on it. "If you stay or want it cleaned to sell it, I'm available. I can even keep an eye on things if you need to go back out of state." She used "out of state" in a sarcastic way that I kind of liked. I put her card in my pocket.

"That could be a great help." I took a slight breath. "Maybe we can grab something to eat later and talk about it. I probably owe you dinner for saving the day with that alarm." She gave me a look of fake shock.

"That would be very nice of you." She seemed genuinely pleased at the invitation. "You stayin' at that new Drury where all the restaurants are? They got some nice ones you could walk to."

I was not sure what any of that implied, but I was interested to find out and somewhat relieved to not have to look for a place to eat in Ferguson. She gave me the name of a restaurant she liked (which I had seen on my way out that morning), and we agreed to meet there at 7. Before she left she showed me how to set the alarm and gave me the code. We shook hands again with her grip noticeably less firm against my palm. I stood on the porch watching her walk back across the street to her house; she turned around at the front door and gave me a little wave that made my heart leap.

Chapter 7

BEN FORD

With my ears still ringing from the alarm, I went inside and closed the door as the silence of the great empty space asserted itself. I felt the loss of my uncle more acutely now that I stood in the house. I looked at the old furniture in his small living room, the sort that a man alone would have picked out 30 years ago. This was his room, but he would never be in it again. There were two large bookcases filled with ideas that had passed through his mind for a time, ideas that may have found roots there, but would no longer bloom out into the world.

Although I expected that there might be a smell there from spoiled milk or something, the place had only a faint odor of Lysol. That, combined with the general lack of dust, made me think that maybe Nicki had plied her trade in the house recently as a gesture of good will. People did things like that sometimes out of a sort of community kindness. When I opened the refrigerator, it was empty except for a six-pack of Budweiser, a couple of regular Cokes, and a box of baking soda.

Something about the empty, made bed, a bed that would probably never be slept in again, kept me from lingering too long in the master bedroom. In the other bedroom was an old table with his not so old

PC on it. I switched it on wondering whether Uncle Al had an internet connection. After it booted up, the wallpaper around which his few icons had been carefully arranged was a picture of my parents from way back in the 80s. They were both laughing as if the photographer had just cracked the funniest joke ever, or maybe they were just incredibly happy. I studied the picture a while wondering if I had ever been that happy or ever would be before clicking on the internet to Google Anna Dare. As I said, I had been living way off the grid for six months and not been too especially interested in the news for several months before that; as the hit numbers approached infinity, I realized just how big a celebrity the woman was. The pictures that popped up showed her at one of the lottery ceremonies, an older woman with an amused look holding a giant check with many zeroes. A caption referred to her as a black woman, but those shining green eyes made me wonder. The titles of the search results told the story of how controversial she was. In a quote she referred to herself as a "woman of colors, many colors."

Anna, the Goddess, The Great Charlatan Named Dare, the Prophet who will Save Us All, Dare the Destroyer. People seemed to either love her or hate her, which is pretty standard for the internet, but everyone agreed that she was important, maybe the most important person on the planet. The diatribes and testimonials were not just from Americans; the whole world had opinions about her. I read one from some guy in Lebanon that struck me.

> **In the Koran there are a series of verses which contain the warning of the fate of the nonbeliever on the Day of Judgement.**
> **Soon I will cast him into Hell-Fire.**
> **And what will explain to you what Hell-Fire is?**
> **Nothing does it permit to endure**

And nothing does it leave alone!
Darkening and changing the color of man.
Over it are the Nineteen.

He went on to explain how the number 19 is so significant. Apparently there are one hundred and fourteen chapters in the Koran which is a multiple of 19. If you add the 12 Imams to God, Adam, Noah, Abraham, Moses, Jesus and Mohammed you also get 19. Apparently, the year after Anna Dare won the second of her two Powerball jackpots, 19 crop circles mysteriously showed up in a 100 mile radius of Saint Louis. The combined winnings of Ms. Dare from both lotteries had been $387,422,521, an exact multiple of 19.

I read many crazy theories with the number of articles supporting or condemning her even though they all seemed to invest her with supernatural powers, either good or evil. The big media outlets were mostly confused by a self-appointed religious leader who never asked for any money, choosing instead to disperse her lottery wealth in unusual ways (she gave a large sum of money to a police officer shot and crippled in the line of duty and sent an equal amount to the family of the man in prison for the shooting). Everyone was impressed by the sales of the book she had written entitled *The Way* which she claimed was a modern Gospel given to her directly by the voice of God. It was a bestseller in 38 countries, even in some where it had been banned. The main thing that news outlets lamented was that Anna Dare would not talk to them. Her only interview was to an independent journalist from Saint Louis named Jill Devereaux who published it in the *Riverfront Times*, a free local paper. I read that interview in its entirety that day and again since I arrived in this place where that issue of the *Times* was on the coffee table along with some *New Yorkers* and a *People* magazine. I am quoting the part that got my attention that day.

Jill Devereaux: Does your belief system make people who adopt it happy?

Anna Dare: If you mean happy in the sense of having every-thing you want, all the time, no. That is not promised, but on the path with God one is happy no matter what the circumstances of life. Peace in the heart requires nothing.

JD: I suppose it is like the old Christian martyrs who were happy even as they were burned at the stake.

AD: I may be able to let you know about that very shortly if some of my critics get their way.

(She laughed then the way people laugh when they have just won something big, the laugh of people who think they have everything)

At some point in the afternoon, I must admit that I decided to check my uncle's email account wondering if the post-it note that said "email password Stendahl57" was correct. It was. All of the unopened mail was spam which made me feel a little less creepy for looking. Still, the creep factor made me want to close it immediately until I noticed some-thing strange. A big load of mail had been deleted leaving a two month gap between the unopened ads and the old emails about his bowling league. Searching through his trash I found one about a month old from adare38@att.net. I printed it out as soon as I figured out how to turn on his old Epson.

Dear Al,
You don't have to give it to me. I really don't care one way or the other. We should at least discuss what you plan to do with it. Stop by soon. You know where I live, postman.
Anna Jacquelline Dare

I could not find a reply to it, and there were no others from her. I looked around the house for a while feeling foolish because I had no idea what I was looking for. An incriminating letter could have been stuck in any one of the many books on the living room shelves. I did open a few and shook them to see if anything obvious fell out, but I didn't really pursue it. I supposed that if someone with as much money as Anna Dare wanted something from a retired mailman, she already had it, which would explain how I had just inherited so much money. I did find a hard copy of the *Riverfront Times next to the bookcase* that had the Jill Devereaux interview, which I took with me.

I will admit that at the time, reading all of the internet controversy surrounding Anna made me want to have nothing to do with her. Her story reminded me of something like Scientology (some of her followers were movie stars), a sort of made up belief. I really had no interest in religion at all, but especially not one referred to constantly as a "cult" by some commentators I had heard of. I just wanted to go to the bank, check on my new money and think about what a sort of date with a woman like Nicki might be like. Turning on the alarm as Nicki had shown me, I left the house to its silence.

Outside, I tried not to look obviously across the street at Nicki's house. I noticed that it had an attached garage and, except for the lawn, seemed to be in good shape. At the time I thought that she might be only renting the place, but it also occurred to me that the apartment in Alabama that still held what could be considered my worldly goods was only a one bedroom with a bed, couch and table all given to me by my employer from a foreclosure.

I walked all around the outside of my uncle's house looking for flaws. I knew that I would sell the property as soon as possible, but the idea of emptying it seemed impossible to consider. I wondered if Nicki knew some trustworthy locals who could take care of it at a reasonable cost. Under the carport, my uncle's Camry sat silently. Even though I had the keys, the idea of driving it or even starting it up gave me the creeps. He had died in it.

Back in my car I placed the email that I had printed out on the passenger's seat wondering if an email from Anna Dare could be worth something by itself. As I sat there, my phone rang. I figured it was my grandfather wanting to tell me about money markets or some old guy thing, but it was a number not in my phone.

"Hey, cuz, heard you were back in town." It was my cousin Erin. She was my mother's older sister's daughter and just about perfect in every way according to the family. She was pretty, perky, and married to some guy who hailed from old Saint Louis money.

"How'd you hear? You talk to grandma every day?" I had never, for obvious reasons, been very close to Erin, even though we were almost the same age. Her parents had always considered me a bad influence, and she had agreed with that assessment.

"No, I don't, but she called me this morning to say that you may have inherited your late uncle's house in beautiful downtown Ferguson. Is that so?"

"Yes. I'm there right now." Erin gave a little gasp.

"Watch yourself, boy." Erin never ventured to any section of the Saint Louis area in which the white population was less than 90%. 'Anyway, I may have a deal for you. I know some people who rehab and flip old houses even in Ferguson. Since they know you are family to me, you'll get a good price, and they will take everything as is. You won't have to do anything with the old stuff that nobody probably wants anyway."

"That would be great." In my whole life, this was the nicest she had ever been to me, and I was touched. Also, the slacker in me just wanted the easiest way out.

"Good. Are you available to meet with them this afternoon? I told this guy you might be going back to Alabama, or wherever, real soon, and he agreed to speed up the process for me. He might even cut you a check today if you two can get together."

"Wow! That sounds perfect." I did not mention that I had no plans to go back to Alabama. My stuff back there seemed tawdry now, and even my new wealth would make any reconciliation with Lisa unlikely. I was thinking about getting a new car that I could drive to a beach to hang out on for a year or so. The money from my uncle's house would be real icing on what was already a nice cake.

"Ok. I just texted him, and he can be there in an hour. Does that work for you?"

"Sure. I just need to go to the bank and do a little business." I was trying to sound as if I was not a total loser.

"Great. Then we can meet for dinner tonight. Just tell me where you want to go, and I'll get a reservation."

"Ok." To be honest, I had always wanted to be close to Erin, so the idea of her inviting me was flattering, until I remembered Nicki. "Ooops, sorry. I've got plans for tonight already."

"Really? Old girlfriend?"

"Something like that." I almost told her it was a woman I had just met in Ferguson, but I did not need the grief or her telling my grandma about it.

"Well, use protection, young single." She laughed at her own joke. "And call me before you go back and we can at least do lunch."

I agreed to do that, and we ended the call with me feeling as if fortune had just decided to smile at me all at once for maybe the first time in my life. I was still basking in that feeling when something strange happened as I looked at the email on my car seat. Just for fun, I counted the letters in "Anna Jacquelline Dare." There are nineteen of them.

Chapter 8

BEN FORD

The bank where my new money waited patiently for me to claim it was just a short drive from my uncle's house back on Florissant Road. When I entered the lobby carrying the file of paperwork the lawyer had provided me, the grim guard standing just inside the door looked me up and down for any bulges that might indicate a weapon. To be honest, I probably needed a haircut (still do) to be categorized as non-threatening in his eyes; I walked over to a teller trying not to make any sudden moves.

"You need to speak to Mr. Hendricks." The teller looked only briefly at my paperwork before pointing at an office in the center of the bank. The guard still had an eye on me as I tapped on the manager's door.

"How may I help you?" Mr. Hendricks was friendly, but also wary since most of the people like me who asked to see him probably had over-drawn accounts. He was about my age, a fact that usually bothered me since he was in a position of authority, and I was still moving furniture. After he went through the paperwork, he seemed quite happy to make my acquaintance. He needed to get some copies of a few things, but was quick to offer me coffee and a donut from a box of Krispy Kremes on his table.

"Thanks." I didn't want one, but took it anyway. He laid the print-outs gently on his desk in front of me.

"Some of these are Certificates of Deposit that still have a few months to go before they fully mature." I chewed my donut before speaking.

"But I could take the money out right now if I wanted to, right?"

"Yes, of course. There would be a small penalty, and unless you needed the money immediately, I would advise against it."

"I'll think about it." I ran a finger up and down those wonderful, big numbers a few times feeling good fortune like a tiny electrical shock. "With these other accounts, is it settled now that I can make a small withdrawal today?"

It was, and I did. The same teller filled out the form for me with a much better attitude. I asked for five hundred bucks with four hundred in impossibly crisp fifties. I knew it was sort of a dopey thing to do, but I needed to feel something in my hands to believe that any of this was happening.

On the way back to my uncle's house I wondered how long I would have to wait for this friend of my cousin which made me consider dropping by Nicki's to chat some more. It turned out that a grey Lincoln was already parked in the driveway, and someone was sitting on his front stoop. The guy, who waved at me as I parked behind him, was dressed casually, but in a new Polo shirt and very clean jeans. He was not a worker.

"Good afternoon, Mr. Ford. I'm Jason Willis, a friend of Erin." He had the firm handshake of a car salesman.

"I hope you weren't waiting too long." Willis had no problem with that and no problem with anything in the house. He walked through the place in three minutes, not stopping one time for a closer look at anything. Even the water heater in the basement, which was old and rusty, did not get a second glance. He had to take a call as soon as we came back upstairs, but was only on for a minute before coming over to me.

"So everything looks great. Would sixty thousand be a fair price for you." I tried unsuccessfully to contain my shock.

"Yes, that seems fair." I may have laughed a little though I tried to control it. "How long do you think it will take?"

"Well, since you are Erin's cousin, I think we can settle this up right now." He pulled a checkbook out of his jeans.

"Oh, sure." The sad truth was that I had never owned any piece of property or consequently sold one. He held out some papers for me to sign which I did though I had a queasy feeling that something was wrong even as I handed him the key. It was all I could do to wait until I was in my car on the way back to the bank to let out a scream of joy. I was so excited to get back to the bank and have a small audience watch me wallow in even more money. Money. Money.

Chapter 9

BEN FORD

At about 6:45 I was standing next to the bar in a restaurant in St. Charles called Prasino's wondering if Nicki would really show up or have second thoughts. I had spoken with the hostess twice to make sure there were still tables available, and I was trying to avoid considering my reflection in the mirrored wall. There was seating for food in the bar area that extended to an outside patio. People my age, people with white-collar jobs still dressed for work, laughed in a carefree way as if they had just closed a big deal. I wished I had worn something other than jeans, but I had packed very light for the trip. I stood apart from them even though I was sure I had made much more money than any one of them had that day. Checking my phone to seem nonchalant about being alone, I noticed it was five after seven. I decided she was not coming for all the plausible and depressing reasons when I heard her call my name.

"Ben! Have you been waiting long? They were doing something on the bridge that slowed it to a crawl." Nicki was not especially dressed up either, but her very tight jeans looked more than good. The back of her red blouse cut in thin strips revealed a glimpse of her naked back. Her dark hair, out of the ponytail, fell nicely on her shoulders, and she had applied some first date make-up though not much. The only odd thing about her outfit were the clunky black shoes, like the old Doc Martens, she was wearing. This could have been a part of her working class persona or it might have meant that she did not want me seeing this as a date at all. I was overthinking things, a tendency that usually ruined any romantic possibilities. I made a gesture toward the restaurant, but she did not follow.

"No let's sit outside in the bar. It is so nice tonight." She turned to a hostess when I nodded my head, and we were directed to a small table on the patio. On the way, we passed a group of young guys who I assumed to be praying, until I realized that their heads were merely bowed toward their phones. The hostess seated us near a big party of young women who seemed to be celebrating a birthday from the number of presents stacked on an empty chair. They had apparently been drinking a while and emitted a cheerful din in all directions. Nicki rolled her eyes at me about the spectacle. When the server came, she ordered a shot of Patron and wagged a long finger toward my forehead. "You up for one?" I said I was.

"It's been kind of a strange day for me." I was going to tell her how gorgeous she looked, but most young women have a problem with compliments that arrive too quickly.

"I bet. Your uncle was a great guy, and he talked about you a lot."

"I feel terrible about not having called him for so long. You said he talked about me?" I was going to add "with you?" to that, but I did not want to be dismissive of her in any way.

"Yep. He worried about you. Especially when he wanted to send you something a few weeks ago. I went on line and found your address in Alabama for him." I probably raised my eyebrows at that.

"I have been having a few rough years." Thinking of my uncle worrying about me, I felt a tear crowd the corner of my eye. I blinked it back and was happy to see the waitress show up with two shot glasses on a tray. She set them down with a sharp click on the tabletop adding a tiny bowl with some slivers of lime between them. Nicki looked around the table as soon as she left and started laughing.

"I can't believe it. No salt shaker." She picked up a lime wedge. "They want us to chug tequila in only the healthiest of ways." She looked straight into my eyes as she held her glass up almost touching her lips. Hoping she did not notice the still lingering tear, I gently touched it with mine being careful not to spill any. She seemed to be thinking of a toast. "Let's down these and then tell each other some personal truth about ourselves that might speed things up one way or the other."

I nodded, and we drank them in one motion. I had not been drinking that much for the last several months to avoid leaning on it too much, so the little explosion in my brain surprised me. Nicki bit into her piece of lime and jammed one into my mouth, one long finger lingering against my lip. I could tell that she was a for sure wild girl, the sort who lived for the moment. I had always avoided such women (probably had something to do with my parents dying in a motorcycle crash when I was ten), but I felt compelled to make the leap. The waiter came back to take our order.

"This is a stupid question, and I apologize in advance for asking." The waitress was looking at Nicki who was glowing now from the tequila. "But those girls at the birthday party wanted me to ask if you are Bella Hadid. I was afraid they would come over themselves and try to get selfies." Nicki threw her head back and laughed.

"Tell them I am, but if they come over my boyfriend will break their button noses." We ordered, and I looked at her again. She was too pretty for me, but she was acting interested using the word "boyfriend" with a sort of familiarity. I had noticed also that her way of speaking had changed since we were standing on a stoop in Ferguson; she was not talking like a girl from the hood so much anymore. I was aware of these facts, but all analysis of them was impossible due to the amazing presence of her.

"Truth time. I'll go first." I was sort of hoping she had forgotten about that. "Mine is that I am biologically incapable of monogamy. When I have feelings for a man, it does not prevent my having feelings for someone else. For me, it's the same as having more than one friend I care about. I seem to have been born this way just like all the Trans and gays and crossdressers and whatever. When nature moves me, desire pours out of me without control. Like that." She snapped her fingers staring again into my eyes.

"That's good to know." My head was spinning. She smiled.

"Some guys like hearing it at first, not so much later." She tapped my hand. "Your turn." I thought those words might be prophetic. Maybe the universe had decided that I might get a turn at what was good in it. Maybe it always happened all at once if you were willing to grab what was in front of you. I took a long breath.

"We may be compatible because I am no good with relationships either." Nicki leaned forward almost imperceptibly. "For my whole life women have seen me as a friend with benefits, someone they could never commit to, never take seriously. And…" I waited a few beats. "That is all fine with me." I said that and immediately wondered whether it was true.

"So you're a fun guy who is not too serious about the world. Girls are fine with the great sex and lack of drama until they get their degrees or start to think about reproducing. Then they move on. Does that sound about right?"

"It sounds terrible, but, yeah, I guess so." Actually, the part about the great sex sounded terrific the way she said it.

"For what it's worth, we may have the exact same story, only I have turned it around to my choice of not wanting to be owned by some man. We may be compatible for sure. Maybe on some other planet we'd be normal." The waiter brought our food.

The burgers were a specialty of the place, and they were big and good. One thing nice about a job like moving furniture was that you could really eat whatever you wanted and burn it off the next day. Nicki ate with great gusto as well devouring her burger with little groans of pleasure. I supposed that cleaning houses all day kept her fit; the muscles in her shoulders seemed as taut as a steel cord. We talked about the food, the girls at the party table who seemed to be taking surreptitious pictures of us, the beauty of the spring evening. When the waiter asked about the check arrangement, I quickly said it was all mine in a tone that implied he was foolish for asking. She smiled to agree that we were on some kind of actual date even gripping my forearm slightly. That is when I saw the bracelet on her wrist. She was wearing what people called "Dare beads," and the people who wore them were part of the Anna Dare cult of the Way. There were four gold charms, each announcing one of the pillars of her belief system. I could see "Accomplish" and "Learn." Noticing my gaze, she rotated the chain around until "Love" and "Joy" showed up.

"You know that your uncle knew Anna Dare, right?" The waitress stopped by just then, and though she seemed anxious to join the conversation, she merely left the check.

"I only just heard." I chose my next words carefully since she was wearing the beads. "I don't know what to think about it or about a lot of things." I told her about Bailey's conspiracy theory about my uncle's death. I was wondering if I was getting too far away from normal date conversation, but she seemed interested.

"The part about the quick cremation and the unexpected inheritance does seem strange. Most people would just look at their bank balance and nothing else." She thought for a minute. "Did this Bailey have a theory about who would want to kill your uncle?"

"He thinks it has something to do with this Anna Dare, but he has nothing but a feeling." She shook her head. "Not that she did anything to him, but that it had something to do with her." She took a sip of water.

"What was the thing he sent to you after I found out where you were living? I asked him why he didn't just look for an email address, and he acted funny about it. Did he say anything about being in any trouble?"

"No, nothing like that. He just sent me something he found of my mother's that she wrote when I was a kid. He thought I'd want to see it I guess." I didn't say that he asked me to call him, which I never got a chance to do.

"That's interesting. What was it?"

"I think it was part of a book she wanted to write. It was sort of a story you tell a kid at bedtime, and it had a strange effect on me." I could feel that there was too much emotion in my voice.

"I'd like to see that some time." Her voice seemed a bit heavy now. "Something like that in your mother's own handwriting would be very special."

"I have it in my hotel room." I was finishing writing the tip on the check as I said this.

"Thank you for dinner." Nicki smiled at me choosing to ignore my veiled invitation as I totaled the amount and scrawled my signature. Maybe she was more of a smart girl than an adventure girl, at least on the first date. As we left the restaurant, I caught some envious looks from guys at the bar. I decided to try another tack.

"Can I walk you to your car?" It was getting dark, and I had some teen idea about a goodnight kiss. She grabbed my arm as we walked outside.

"I would really like seeing that letter your uncle sent you if you feel like showing it to me." She directed this as a whisper toward my cheek. I agreed quickly in an enthusiastic way that made her laugh aloud. It was the sort of laugh I had not heard in a while.

Chapter 10

BEN FORD

It felt wonderful, a way of feeling I had almost forgotten about, to enter the hotel lobby with Nicki clinging firmly to my arm. I remember her laughing at something I said as we cruised by the front desk causing two older business travelers to give me a look of envy, or at least I felt that look strong enough to make it real. We had to wait a long 30 seconds for the elevator to arrive and take us to my third floor room, and the brief interlude paused our conversation as we focused on the slow drip of the light moving toward our floor.

"Alone at last!" She said this one second after the elevator door oozed shut and two seconds before we kissed. I can't really say that I made the first move, though I started to, as her face launched toward mine at the same time colliding with fervor that I had never experienced before. If I was thinking about it (I wasn't), I would have been nervous about heading up to a hotel room with someone I just met. Girls who are into hookups are usually not into me, but I was not thinking about anything but getting to the room. We were still kissing as the door opened; Nicki stuck her foot out to keep it from closing while we continued.

We emerged from the elevator dazed and laughing and hot. Walking down the long hallway, I spied a guy bent over by the door of the room across from mine fiddling with his key card and having some kind of problem. I briefly considered helping him out with it, just to get him out of the hallway and into his room before we went into mine, but did not. Nicki stood just behind me as I unlocked my door, her hand resting on the back of my thigh. Just as the green light indicated a successful connection, I heard a sound that seemed very wrong, a sort of moan that combined shock and fear being squeezed out of Nicki's mouth simultaneously.

"Get in there now, fast!" This was spoken by a man's deep voice, the guy who had been trying to unlock his door. He had the authoritative voice of a policeman, a voice trained to be immediately obeyed, and I quickly pushed the door open and stumbled in. When I turned around, I saw that he had one hand firmly clutching Nicki's throat while the other held a large gun pressed against her ear.

"Step back and just listen now." He was calm, but there was malice in his tone as he pushed the door shut with his butt. I backed up until my calves touched the big king bed. "You need to do exactly what I say when I say it. You are in control of whether your little girl here gets hurt or not. You got that?"

I nodded. In retrospect it was not a bad way for him to have handled the situation, shifting the fight or flight hormones that seemed to be flowing into my limbs as if from a fire hose to focus on just following his orders to prevent a horror from erupting in the room. I am certain that before that moment in my life, the world had never reversed itself so completely before, from the joy of drawing each breath to the dread of never drawing another in a few seconds. Releasing his hand from Nicki's throat, he pulled something from his coat pocket and tossed it on the bed. It was handcuffs.

"Please, no." Nicki was starting to plead and the words came out like a sob.

"Shut the fuck up!" The man with the gun said this firmly, but I could tell he thought she was losing it the way he started talking fast. "Now you're going to get face down right here on the floor with your hands behind your back, and your boyfriend is going to slip those cuffs on you nice and easy." He winked at me as if we were in this together, just two buds getting our kicks tying up a woman. "You're gonna be my good girl now and let this happen so you can stay all pretty."

"God. I'm so scared. I can't breathe." She was shaking now, on the edge of hysterics. Instantly, he turned the gun away from the right side of her head in order to deliver a hard slap to her left temple. I anticipated that violence, and it did not surprise me. What did surprise me was the impossible speed of Nicki's arms and legs and torso as she went into an elaborate dance of her own violence. Her head slammed backward into his nose, her big shoe found his shin while her fingers did something to his hand that held the gun. I was about to jump in, but two seconds after she started she held his gun pointed straight at his chest. Her voice changed.

"Don't do anything that will make me pull this trigger because I really, really want to." She barely opened her mouth when she spoke. "Now let's just do what I say, and the poor hotel maid won't have to clean up a big fucking mess." She convinced him that she was serious. She convinced me too. Keeping the gun pointed at him, she made him get on the floor face down. She put the barrel on the back of his head as she went through his pockets.

"We should call the cops." That seemed like a reasonable thing for me to say, but she shook her head.

"I don't think so. Our friend here probably was one until a couple years ago. Maybe some of his old pals would answer the call." She pulled out something from one of his pockets. "Well, lookee what we got here. Throw me those cuffs."

"Nicki…" I set the cuffs down on the floor by her trying to think of something to say to make her calm down.

"Put your hands behind your back like a perp. There you go." Immediately she jammed the thing she had found into his neck making a brief spark as the man went into convulsions. Setting down the gun, she snapped the handcuffs on his wrists and lay down next to him, their noses almost touching.

"Ain't no fun bein' tased, is it, my man?" He said nothing as the spit rolled down his chin. She let him see the device in her hand and moved it closer and closer to his face until he answered.

"No."

"That's right. Now how many people waiting for you downstairs?"

"Two." He answered as fast as he could.

"Nicki, this is nuts." I think I still thought I could calm her down.

"If I was you, I'd be packing up my shit right now." She didn't wait for an answer turning back to the man on the floor. I did start throwing stuff into my case because I couldn't think of anything else to do, and I was still trying to avoid being at a murder scene. "Where they waitin'?" Her accent had reverted to the one I had heard in Ferguson.

"In a van just outside the back door." She thought a minute.

"You done packin'? You got everything?" I started stuffing things in faster. "Give me a pair of your underwear, preferably worn, and rip the sheet off the bed." She was up now removing one of the pillowcases. I handed her the pair of underwear that she jammed into the man's mouth tying the twisted pillowcase around his head to hold it into place. Making the sheet into a long rope, she threaded it through his cuffed hands before tying it around the desk with a knot I had never seen before. She removed another pillowcase before placing it over the man's head. She took my hand and lead me to the door pausing to peep out before she opened it. She put the "Do Not Disturb" sign on, and we took off down the hall.

"Let's at least call the cops when we get to the lobby." I was still thinking about the remaining two guys in the van.

"No cops just yet." She still held the gun in both hands as we walked. "We need to find another hotel where we can hold up for the night."

"OK." To be honest, I was not thinking straight, and the trip down the stairs (she shook her head at the elevator) was surreal with the heavy echo of our footsteps. Nicki pulled the silencer off as we descended.

"We want this thing loud if we have to use it." She smiled as she said this, and something about the look in her eyes and her statement about spending the night somewhere made me go along when all my instincts told me to stop in the lobby and tell the desk clerk what had happened.

"My car is this way in the garage." We were walking fast through the lobby in the opposite direction, the gun now in the front of her jeans with her shirt pulled over it.

"Let's take mine. It's right out here in the open which is way better than going into a parking garage with only one exit."

Her car was a bright red Challenger SRT Demon. I did not know what that was until she told me. I have never been much into cars, but I noticed a group of young guys checking it out as we weaved through the parking lot. With the new smell of the leather interior in my nostrils, I might have wondered how someone cleaning houses could afford it, but the sight of the pistol now stuck in the drink cup holder was strange enough to quash any questions. We soon pulled hard onto the ramp of Highway 70.

"Buckle up." I did that just as Nicki goosed the engine into giving out a dangerous roar, easily zipping in front of a semi before crossing three lanes of traffic. The wide Missouri went by in a flash. The speedometer said 90, and her laughter was mostly a scream.

Chapter 11

YATES

"I'm going to stop you there, young man." Yates spoke with his head back and his eyes closed. He opened them to look at Ryan at an angle. "Any ideas who this thug was or which of the many psycho groups around the country he has a membership in? Does Ford make any accusations?" Ryan started to answer, but Milla cut him off.

"I think we should listen to this story exactly as it's told." She got up to walk to the bar. "That was your idea, and I believe it was Anna Dare's idea as well."

"Anna Dare." Yates said the name in the same way he might say the name of his ex-wife: with irony and regret. Ryan felt uncomfortable.

"Sir, I would remind you again that we have no way of verifying any of the facts presented here at this time." Part of being a lawyer was an ability to make the same statement over and over until it was accepted. He could tell he would have to say it again as Yates was not listening to him.

"Show me some pictures of Bella Hadid." Yates queried the computer system in a sharp voice. In an instant, the monitor on the wall showed a glamorous woman in a red mini-skirt getting out of a limousine. Yates stared at the picture intensely. "Could there be a woman who looks like that cleaning houses and kicking asses in Ferguson, Missouri?"

"I believe there are beautiful women in states other than California and New York." Milla fixed herself a Pellegrino holding up the bottle to Ryan as a way of asking if he wanted one. He said no thanks.

"Yes, but they all go there as soon as they can buy a ticket out of Dogpatch." Yates winked at Milla who had told Ryan once that her hometown was Wichita. "And explain to me why such a woman would take any interest in this dumb, what is he, a furniture mover?" Yates was happy. He enjoyed feeling that he saw through things. "Why, indeed?"

"Anna Dare would say that the worth of one man cannot be calculated by another. Actually, she said exactly that in her book." Milla ordered the computer to stop the slide show of Bella Hadid photographs that had begun to show the model posing in various bikinis.

"Anna probably did say that, but I am sure that she feels that her own worth is quite above reproach." Milla did not acknowledge the comment as she was checking some message on her phone before texting something with the insouciance of a woman who considers herself beyond reproach. Ryan took note and imagined that he would be preparing a prenup for her signature very shortly.

"Please read on, Mr. Monahan. Let's see if these people are worthy of our interest." Milla trailed a hand across Yates' back as she walked around the sofa to sit down. He picked up the document and cleared his throat experiencing a decidedly unprofessional thrill at being about to read the next section to Milla. She had asked for it.

Chapter 12

BEN FORD

We had slowed back down somewhere close to the speed limit when Nicki took out her phone and instructed it to call the Hilton in Frontenac, that tony suburb of Saint Louis. In yet another voice, she told the person who answered a long story about being on her honeymoon and being "appalled" by the "accommodations" she had booked. Would they possibly have anything at all available at any price? They did, and we again shot across three lanes of Highway 70 to pull off on Lindbergh. We slowed down to what seemed to be a crawl, and she squeezed my thigh gently.

"You ok, hon?" She did not turn to look at me, her eyes darting from the road to the rearview mirror as if on a timer.

"Are you some kind of a martial arts instructor or something on the side?" I thought about putting my hand on top of hers, but, to be honest, at that point the normal things did not seem appropriate.

"Something like that. I studied it a little." She still did not look at me. She froze for a second, and her eyes went wide as a car tore out of a side street behind us, but she immediately decided it was no threat. I stared at her profile wondering whether such a woman could actually have any interest in me. There was still my inheritance, but I doubted that would impress her for long. To avoid creeping her out by staring, I turned my gaze to the road. I had not been on this north part of Lindbergh for many years. We were passing the site of the old Northwest Plaza Shopping Center, which had once been the largest in the world, if you believed my grandma. It had closed up a while ago and now looked like a set from some dystopian movie. Although there was some traffic, the area seemed more deserted and sadder than Ferguson with the little stores in the strip malls lighted more to deter theft than attract customers. We passed a shop called "Secret Desires" that existed there because there was no surrounding citizenry who cared enough about sex toy sales to run them off. The street, however, improved with every mile, slowly giving way to nicer stores, fancier office space, better condos, cooler cars at the stoplights, and the sweet smell of material satisfaction culminating in Frontenac, where Lindbergh really became lucky.

"Here we be." Nicki pulled into the parking lot of the Hilton choosing a space way in the back. "Just let me act like some rich bitch who wants to do all the talking, ok?" I nodded as I watched her put the gun back under her blouse. I stood there mostly mute as she went through the check-in with a very efficient woman who was Indian or Pakistani. She paid for the room, which was the most expensive I had ever stayed in, with her own American Express.

"I will detest having to change my name on all of my cards, but he is very worth the inconvenience." She wiggled the fingers on her left hand, which sported a diamond ring that I had not noticed earlier. The woman smiled in a way that seemed both admiring and conspiratorial.

"Will you be needing any assistance with your luggage?" I started to point to my backpack to imply that I was good.

"Thank you, but we will see the room before we unload the car.

We've already done that once this evening." She did sound like a young executive, polite, but entitled to the best at all times. When the clerk handed her over the key, I saw the same Dare bead bracelet as Nicki wore slide down her wrist, the word "Learn" stopping just short of her little finger.

Unlocking another hotel room door with Nicki, I was nervous, but she stood with her back against mine watching the hallway. Once inside she did a brief tour of the room looking in the shower and even under the bed before plopping on the little sofa and kicking off her heavy shoes with a thud. I stood in the middle of the room holding my backpack.

"Relax. I think we are good here. Way less crazies in this part of town." I didn't move.

"So what do you think just happened, and why didn't we call the cops and get that guy arrested?" I had been in shock, I guess, but I was coming out of it. These questions had been rattling around in my head all the way down Lindbergh. "They will find that guy in my hotel room, you know." She pulled off her socks and put her bare feet on the coffee table right next to the gun; her toenails were bright purple, in contrast to her colorless fingernails.

"I'm not sure what happened, but I am sure nobody will find that guy in your room. His buddies already found him and took off." She patted the cushion next her beckoning me to sit down. "They a lot of fanatics in the area nowadays, folks coming from all over, and they both for and against Anna Dare." I sat next to her letting my backpack slide to the floor.

"But I have nothing to do with any of this. I barely heard of Anna Dare before this morning. I don't know anything about her." I could see now the red mark on her left cheek where the thug had slapped her. I wondered if it would turn into a bruise. "My uncle knew her, I think, but not me."

"Yeah, he knew her alright. I don't know how, but he did." She put a finger on her cheek, maybe checking for swelling. "You really been off the grid down in Alabama. Anna Dare's a big deal."

"I read about it on the web at my uncle's."

"Yeah, well, she's got tons of haters and haters of those haters, some of them ready to do crazy violent shit." She tapped the gun with her big toe.

"I am thinking my uncle had something on the Dare woman, something from back in the day. He used to be a mailman in Ferguson, and those guys know a lot of what's going on." She touched my shoulder. I was wondering if this was a good time to take up where we left off in the elevator.

"Can I see the thing he sent you? The letter we were going to look at before we got distracted by sex and violence." I picked up the backpack and set it on the coffee table unzipping the side pocket. As I pulled out the paper a box of condoms that I had bought at a Walgreen's on the way back from my uncle's, popped into view for a second before I stuffed them back down. Nicki read my uncle's letter and my mother's old bedtime story without appearing to have noticed them.

"Wow! That's a beautiful memory from your mom. How old were you when she died?"

"Almost ten. She and my dad at the same time on the same motorcycle."

"Yeah, your uncle told me about that." She moved her feet from the coffee table to place them onto my lap. "I'm just gonna say something here about Anna Dare. She changed my life with that book she wrote. I don't know if Anna is all she says she is, but what she said did something to me. My life seemed to me to be worthless, and now I think it has some point to it. That's a big thing no matter what."

"I get that. I do." I didn't. I was coming out of one kind of shock, but about to go into another. The gentle weight of her legs and nearness of her bare feet were almost too much to bear.

"Here's the thing. I think some people are thinking you know something about Anna, whatever your uncle knew, and they either want you to hurt her or stop you from doing it. That's why they wanted to have a conversation with you in that van. See what you be knowing."

"Maybe I really should go see the cops." She shook her head.

"All cops do is clean up the mess after somebody is dead unless they get lucky, and the shooter's car won't start, and he's right outside the house waitin' for them. They don't do much before shit happens. Ask all the sisters who tell the cops their exes are fixin' to murder them, and then they go ahead and do it."

"Maybe I just need to get out of town for a while until this blows over." I sort of meant that, but I also wanted to see her reaction to me going away.

"Or." She dragged that word out to four syllables. "We could try to find out what your uncle had on Anna and give it to her. She would probably make it worth our while the way she writes the big checks." In a single fluid motion, she slid onto my lap facing me. "What you think about that?"

I was not thinking about anything other than her right then, not about the stupidity of getting involved in a dangerous game, not about the possibility that she might be using me, not about her membership in a cult, not that she might be a terrible force to unleash into my life. I just wanted her. We went at it passionately, just like in the elevator with her convincing me that not much else mattered in the universe, but what we were doing. She was biting my ear hard when she stopped and whispered into it.

"Show me that box of rubbers you got in your pack." I reached over and pulled them out with what I hoped was a sexy flourish. She looked at the package and smiled.

"Super lubricated?" Now she laughed hard. "These be great when you fuck my auntie, but I think I'm way slick enough just now." She tossed the box to the floor. "So I ain't worried about bareback if you ain't, seeing as how I recently had a gun against my head for a long minute."

I readily agreed with that, and she sprang from my lap. At the foot of the bed, she undressed slowly, eyes closed, as if following the beat of a slow song playing in her head. I took my clothes off as well trying to feel the rhythm in the same way, but keeping my eyes wide open. When we were both naked, I took her into my arms and kissed her until she shoved me back onto the large Hilton bed. Just before she joined me, Nicki moved the pistol to the nightstand.

"You never know about tomorrow, so let's not hold one thing back for later." I reached to pull her to me, but she was already there.

Chapter 13

BEN FORD

In the earliest part of the next morning I opened my eyes to find the most beautiful woman I had ever made love to (or seen close up) lying inches away from me. I was looking at her back, and she was texting or doing something on her phone with my uncle's will open in the space between us. There were no flaws anywhere that I could detect with each vertebra of her spine a diamond suddenly unearthed with each breath she took. I said nothing, being quite content to keep Nicki in that perfect state of someone so desirable who also desired me. (If you are reading this, Nicki, and I hope you are, I apologize for telling everything. It just feels right to hold nothing back.)

My feelings were even more intense because of the nature of the sex we had experienced. There was none of the awkwardness of first times with the tenuous caresses that were always sensitive to what might be unacceptable. My last girlfriend in Alabama had stopped me just before we were about to make love initially to recite a litany of preferred and taboo behavior. Nicki, on the other hand, seemed to want exactly what I wanted in the identical amount like some fantasy come to life. I put my hand on her hip to convince myself she was real. She did not jump, but set down her phone and straightened her leg.

"Hey, sleepy. You ready for round four?" She turned toward me biting my arm. "I need some breakfast, sugar, or I'll rip the flesh off your bones."

"You been doing some light reading?" I tapped the will that she was now lying on.

"We got no secret places between us after last night, do we, baby?" She moved her hands freely over my body as if it were her own. "You ever heard of this Miss Dixon before? Your uncle talk about her?"

"I never heard him mention her."

"Well, I think I found her."

"How?" We kissed then for a while so that when she answered I was not sure what question she was answering.

"I know people who know how to find people. She is in a nursing home a ways from here."

I began to explore her as well. "Can I ask you something?"

"Anything."

"Were you really a self-defense instructor?" She laughed and rolled away from me.

"I was almost a Navy Seal once until I washed out a month before graduation, so that teaches you a thing or two about hand to hand combat and how to be cool around weapons." She didn't seem to want to expand on that, and I let it go. She stood up and stretched her hands as high above her head as she could. Her body was really toned like a dancer or serious swimmer or maybe an almost Navy Seal.

"I could use a shower. You want to wash my back, boy?"

"I do." She turned around.

"On the other hand, maybe you should make me squeal one more time while I am still all dirty. You up for that?"

"I am." Nicki jumped back onto the bed pushing the will to the floor.

"I like your attitude, sailor." She kissed me. "Let's do it and go see what this Mr. Dixon did for your uncle's money." Only after we showered and grabbed some coffee and breakfast sandwiches from the restaurant did I ask where we were going.

"Way down to the boot heel of Missouri, son. She's in a home in some town called Steele that I never heard of. At least nobody will be looking for us there. All these real crazies stay close around Anna Dare in case the Rapture starts happening."

"You're sure this is the right Miss Dixon?"

"You got to trust me, big man." I almost spilled my coffee as she jerked the Challenger onto Highway 64. Siri calmly gave directions as Nicki checked the rearview mirror occasionally. Although this seemed like a useless trip, and I would have normally asked to be taken back to get my abandoned car, nothing seemed normal at that point. My old friends from college had always made fun of me for getting too involved with women too quickly, giving them all the power right at the beginning of a relationship, a practice that kept them from taking me seriously. It didn't matter. I was falling hard for Nicki, and I didn't care where we were going.

"You think that guy last night had something to do with this Anna Dare?" Her eyes left the road for just a second.

"I don't know. I saw that email in your backpack from her to your uncle. Old Al had something she wanted, and anything she wants is worth big bucks. That psycho thought you had it."

"Maybe it's in the house. There are lots of places to hide things even in a little house like that. I never really looked."

"I don't think he would have kept that in the house." She seemed convinced of that, and I was wondering if she was just trying to make me feel better.

"Good thing. Cause I sold his place and everything in it to some guy my cousin recommended. It's all his now."

"That's interesting, isn't it? You get a good price?"

"Yup." I wanted to brag a bit. "With that money and what I already got from my uncle, I am kind of stupid rich for me. For most people." I touched her cheek gently. "So maybe I don't care about finding this thing, whatever it is, if there's a risk involved. Maybe we should just go to the beach."

"Ain't no risk where we goin'. All them crazies are back there like I said." She flicked her head toward the rear of the car. "If this is just a goose chase, we can get you back to your car, and you can be on your way." I did not like how casual she was about me driving out of her life. I was wondering what it would take to change her mind.

"Should we put the gun in the glove compartment?" It was back in the drink cup holder, pointing forward.

"Nope." Nicki's hands on the steering wheel were quite beautiful. Her nails were cut short for housecleaning, but her elegant fingers tapping in time to a song in her head mesmerized me. She noticed me staring, I think, and tapped the side of my head. "Just relax and find us some tunes."

"Ok, just don't get us a ticket." She thought about that statement a bit.

"Yeah, I get it. Losing my momma and daddy in an accident would make me cautious, too. Shit like that is hard to get through, I bet."

"It was a long time ago, now. I remember we had a huge blowout that New Year's Eve for the millennium. They made a big deal out of it, which was cool because it was our last one."

"You made your peace with it?" This was a question with only the slightest bit of inflection to keep it from being a statement.

"You have to, I guess." I was pretty sure that wasn't true, but I could tell she preferred me to be beyond it. I do want to be beyond it and not struggling to blame all of my failures on that one unfortunate event.

"Um hmm." She said this not in a way that doubted my sincerity, but more suggesting that she understood that misery, even when endured, could never be completely forgotten. She took my hand and kissed each finger. She was driving me crazy.

"Listen, we can do this, even though this lady might be too senile to know anything." She smiled at the heaviness in my voice. "But maybe we should just keep going afterward and forget about all of this. My uncle left me a lot of money that we can live on for a long time."

"Live on?"

"Yes. We could live anywhere. You could start another business and just hire people to clean for you." I had no idea what I was saying. "We wouldn't have to do anything for a year, just travel around, wherever you want to go." She kissed my hand again.

"That's a nice little proposal, I guess, but you remember me sayin' who I am? I won't do well being the property of anyone, even the sweetest man on the planet, which you just might be." She released my hand. "I'm just that way. My momma was the same, but she never knew it. That's what did her in. Fuck!"

The last word referred to flashing lights behind us from a rapidly approaching cop car. It turned out to be State Police gliding past us on their way to something else. She moved the gun under the seat and used the distraction to change the subject.

"By the way, I checked the web, and there was no report of nothing from your hotel last night. So our boy got out of there like I thought before the maid found him."

I supposed that was a good thing since the room was in my name, but the idea of that guy coming after me made me nervous. I started looking out the window at what she told me were cotton fields. I never knew they had the stuff in Missouri, but I had not spent much time in the southern part of the state. Because I had not had any real sleep the night before, the little flecks of white in the fields rolling past put me to sleep. I was sort of dreaming when her tongue flipped across my ear to wake me.

"We're here, I think." I opened my eyes to see a dingy looking building with a sign on the front that said Colonial Gardens. Three old women sat on a wooden bench to the side of the front door watching us as we got out of the car. A bored receptionist with a wolf head tattooed on her forearm gave us Mrs. Dixon's room number. Just as we started down the hall, she called us back and pointed toward the dayroom where a woman in a wheel chair was working on a jigsaw puzzle. She took us over to her.

"Mr. Dixon, you have some visitors."

"Do I?" She looked a little confused and nervous as if she should know who we were, but could not place us. She was really old. The receptionist left us alone.

"Yes, ma'am. My name is Ben Ford. My uncle was…"

"Albert!" She seemed very proud of herself to beat me to his name. For some reason I couldn't think of anything to say. Nicki jumped in clutching the old woman's hand.

"We didn't know whether you knew, Miss Dixon, but he passed a few weeks ago." She squeezed Nicki's hand back and smiled. Everyone likes beautiful women.

"Yes, that lawyer called me, the one from Ferguson, to send me a check or something. I don't remember now if he was going to mail it or bring it himself. I thought you might be him." Nicki dropped to one knee beside the wheelchair.

"We'll call him when we get back to Saint Louis. Would you prefer it mailed?"

"Oh, it makes no difference to me. Not even sure what I would spend money on." She looked around. "Maybe some better puzzles." Mrs. Dixon found her own joke to be hilarious and giggled if an old woman can giggle. We talked a while. It turned out that she had been my uncle's high school teacher way back in the 50s, the one he credited for putting him on the path to lifetime learning. They had stayed in touch even after she retired and moved to Steele to take care of her mother.

"Albert came to see you pretty often, did he?" Nicki was using yet another voice I had not heard, the soothing voice of a nurse about to remove a catheter.

"He visited me several times a year, God bless him, always bringing a pie or flowers or some nice thing to brighten my day." She was smiling, but I was afraid that she might start sobbing any minute.

"He was a good man in so many ways." She hugged the old woman gently. "You must have seen him just before he died. He said something about coming down here, I think."

"Yes, I think so, not long ago, a month or so maybe." She was thinking about it. "Yes, he brought me that strange big bear."

"A teddy bear?" Nicki's face betrayed nothing, but I think mine did.

"The biggest one I had ever seen. He said something about it keeping me company, and made me promise that it would stay in my room with me." She laughed. "I think he thought I might give it away because I usually give things away." Nicki reached over and took my hand suddenly overcome by emotion.

"Oh, my. No, I couldn't ask."

"Ask what?" Nicki had spoken to me, but Mrs. Dixon sensed that she was suddenly significant and longed to understand why.

"It's just that our daughter Aubrey has this great love of teddy bears and also loved her great, great uncle so very much." She paused to collect her emotions. "I'm so sorry. I could never ask."

"Everyone should ask, dear, or they will never get anything." Mrs. Dixon pulled back the sleeve of her bulky sweater to reveal a Dare bead bracelet surrounding the blue veins of her thin wrist. "Of course your daughter should have it, even if we didn't have matching bracelets." She had seen Nicki's.

"We would pay you for it, of course." Nicki looked at me like a wife who had made a decision her husband had better go along with. I nodded. The old woman laughed.

"I think I am already getting a pot full of money when this lawyer gets around to sending it, more that I will be able to spend in what is left to me of life." She flipped the beads of the bracelet. "It will be a great pleasure to give it to your little girl, and I don't get many great pleasures these days." I felt Nicki's nails dig into my shoulder as we pushed Miss Dixon down the hall to her room. It was private, but tiny with only a small bed and two folding chairs around a card table. On one side there was an oak shelf filled with books that was way too big for the room. On top of it with its head touching the ceiling was the big purple bear, the sort you try to win at a carnival. We stood there looking at it.

"You will have to get on a chair to get it down. Your uncle put it up there so high, I think, to keep me from giving it away or something."

I moved one of the chairs over to the bookcase and plucked the stuffed animal down handing it to my adoring wife Nicki who cradled it in her arms like a child. I felt bad that Mrs. Dixon felt so moved by the gesture making an "Aw" sound.

"I am so happy to be able to give this to someone that dear Al loved. He was such a good boy and became a better man." She was almost going to cry at the thought.

We thanked her and said some other things without heaping on too many more lies and left her there. Nicki carried the big bear herself still hugging it to her chest as we went down the hall, past the bored receptionist, past the three old ladies on the porch to the Challenger. Once we shut the car doors, she let out a little shriek, but none of the women heard it.

Chapter 14

BEN FORD

"There is something inside this little monster. You can tell the seam has been sewed up." Nicki pointed to the spot, and I started tearing at it wondering whether she could be right. "Hold on, psycho. We need to find a mall or some place that sells some fancy cutting instruments. No telling what's in here, so we need to be careful. Besides, I need to get some underwear and shit. I've been going commando all damn day."

Siri located a Wal-Mart in Cape Girardeau that was on the way back. I waited in the car with the bear on my lap to the thrill of some little kids that went by, but probably not their mothers who gave me a suspicious look. To pass the time I searched on my phone for houses that could be rented on the beach for a couple of months. I thought that might be a good start. I still imagined that Nicki and I could find a life together even though we had just met. Everything seemed to have changed in the world now, and I had some vague hopes that all of it, especially with what was in the bear, added up to a new chance at life for me.

"You textin' your girlfriend, player?" Nicki must have seen me messing with the phone though I had put it away when she opened the door.

"Nope just thinking about moving to the beach for a while and watch the waves roll in and out. How's that sound?"

"Too bad you sold that house in Ferguson so quick. Little Aubrey was looking forward to living there."

"Imaginary girls can live anywhere."

"They sure can." She was looking up something on her phone. "Let's run up here to this motel and perform a little surgery on Teddy in private."

It wasn't long before we were sitting on the bed in a Hampton Inn with the stuffed bear between us. Nicki used a box cutter to slice easily through the back of it before slowly opening the rest with some heavy sewing scissors. I kissed her hand gently as she worked.

"Easy, boy. I don't want to go too far too quick. Besides, no romance until you feed me first. I'm fixin' to starve, so watch I don't take a bite out of you."

"Feel free." Just then, she began to spread the bear open with her long fingers. She lay it face down and slowly pulled the guts out of it. Sticking her hand inside, she twisted a large object in a plastic bag until it was free.

"See! We ain't crazy." Nicki put the package in front of my face. Even though some of the stuffing still clung to it, I could see that inside the bag was a spiral notebook, a thick five-subject thing that looked old and withered. She removed it slowly and set it on the bed. That's when I saw words written in faded marker ink on the cover. "A Book of Revelations by Val and Jack Ford." I think I gasped.

"Your parents?"

"Yes. At least those were their names."

"Here's a date." She pointed to an inscription that read "1993" in a sort of calligraphy. Nicki flipped through it quickly, but gently to avoid tearing a page. "There's two handwritings here. The one is like the piece your uncle sent you, but there is another." She held open a page. "Is this your dad's?" I stared at the tortured cursive in front of me that was straight up and down with all the incomplete loops on the f's and g's. I felt the pit of loss open up inside me, one that I thought I had closed forever.

"I think so." I covered my eyes with my hands hoping that I didn't cry. Nicki said nothing for a while, just held my wrist.

"It's a hard thing to appear so sudden." She tapped the notebook. "But you have both of your parent's voices right here. Most people never really hear them when they are alive, and they never get another chance."

"That's true." Turning the book so I could read it, I shook my head to prevent any tears from dropping out. The back part contained more of the short poems my mother had written. At the beginning, after a Roman numeral "I," my father had written a strange opening sentence. "Whether you believe it or not, we have felt the presence of God in the Universe this year and have been shown The Way."

"Well, well." Nicki ran a finger over that sentence.

"What?"

"As far as I can tell, this is a draft, and not too rough of a draft, of Anna Dare's book that has sold like a billion copies all over the world since she published it a couple years ago."

"So my parents wrote her book back in the 90s? Fuck. Anna Dare plagiarized it. No wonder she wants it, no wonder everyone wants it." I had seen her slim book in drug stores and at the counter of filling stations without paying much attention to it.

"Looks like they wrote it all right, but you would have a hard time proving it unless they had published it or established some legal record."

She held it up and shook the notebook in case some piece of paper might fall out. "Your uncle, of course, knew it was real. I can't think what he planned to get out of it though."

"Damn. Do you think he was blackmailing her, and she got some of her followers to get rid of him?"

"Nah, he didn't seem like the type to do no crimes, and Anna is all about the love." I forgot for a minute that she was wearing Dare beads. She kept paging through the notebook studying my parent's words.

"So what do we do?" I ran my hand up her leg.

"We go eat at a restaurant in town here that faces the river, and then we come back and get freaky on each other." She kissed me in that way she did where her mouth became the softest, most welcoming place in the world. Her lips held my upper lip tightly for a long time. "Now let me change into something nice I bought while you go buy me one of those big tote bags they was selling in the lobby." She held up the notebook. "We ain't leaving this here alone."

I followed her instructions and found the small shop that sold t-shirts, hats, coffee mugs, and shot glasses that would show people I had been to Cape Girardeau, Missouri. There were tote bags as well, and I flipped through them lazily. All of the alarm bells about Nicki were going off, but I wasn't listening to them. Some part of me thought she might actually be gone when I got back to the room, off to make her own deal now that she had the notebook. That same part of me maybe wanted her to leave me right then before I fell even more deeply in whatever I was in with her. That is how losers think, folks.

"There's some different bags over there that aren't Cape bags." The older woman who ran the shop must have thought that I didn't like such touristy things. I went over to the table by the window to look at the others that were nicely made with huge bursts of color running through them. I picked up one with an odd blend of orange and gray when I noticed the word "Learn" stitched in small block letters at the bottom. The next had "Accomplish" running all along the side. I held it up to the woman.

"Anna Dare inspired?" She smiled.

"Of course. My daughter makes them." She held one up almost caressing it. "She was in a bad way with the drugs and everything a year ago when somebody gave her that book, and it changed her. I don't know how, but I don't question a miracle that saved my sweet girl." The actual tears in her eyes made me just nod and buy a purple and yellow bag without saying anything else. In the hallway back to the room I walked slowly, preparing myself for the emptiness I would find. Maybe there would be a note, but probably not.

"Voila." Nicki was standing in the middle of the room when I opened the door. She was wearing a bright yellow sundress with very thin straps. There were also thin straps on the yellow sandals that wrapped around her ankles, which I noticed when she did a little twirl. "Hard to believe what you can buy at the Wal-Mart." I nodded, but it was all I could do to not fall to my knees.

'I'm not hungry."

"Too bad, boy. I need some food." She took the tote from me placing the notebook, her phone, a small purse, and the handgun inside. She regarded the design. "It's pretty."

"It's an Anna Dare bag. I thought that would be appropriate." I pointed to word "Pleasure" at the top. She squealed.

"That's perfect. Jesus, she's everywhere." She slipped it over her bare shoulder. "By the way, we should know something real quick like about how much this thing is worth."

"How's that?"

"I just sent a text to Anna herself telling her what we had." I laughed.

"Oh, that's great. Why didn't I think of that?" I said this just as we were at the door where she gave me another one of those long kisses.

"I'm serious as a heart attack, boy." She wiped some lipstick from my mouth with her finger. "Didn't I tell you that I clean house for Anna? You have to be able to text the boss."

Chapter 15

YATES

"Well, well, it's a good yarn, isn't it? Tell me, Ryan. Would you ever write so candidly about your sexual adventures with a woman you are supposedly in love with or is that too personal a question?"

The afternoon light in the room was still strong though a few plump clouds had floated into the sky while he was reading, one of which was just then dulling the sun. Ryan stared out at the still gorgeous view for a few seconds wondering if the question was one that he could ignore. The look on Yates' face suggested it was not.

"I probably would not write about it, but some people are very open about such things these days."

"Ah, you young people posting your intimacies on the internet and then wondering how everything about you is known." He included Ryan and Milla with his sweeping hand gesture. She squinted at the document in Ryan's lap as if trying to discern how much remained.

"It seems that Ben has been inspired to tell the whole truth about himself and leave nothing out. It may be that Anna inspired him." For the first time that day, she appeared restless.

"Good old Anna." Yates thought for a second before continuing. "Why would she want this written if it exposes her as a complete fraud or at least implies that she stole the whole holy book from someone else? The book is the thing that people love her for, isn't it? Is she as crazy as they are saying?" Yates was genuinely upset now having said these thoughts aloud. "And why give me this information now, information that I could easily use to discredit her at any time?" Ryan decided to say what he had been thinking since the day before.

"There is some evidence in this document, if it is determined to be factual, which suggests that Ms. Dare may be suffering from some form of mental illness." Ryan wanted to project that he had a firm grip on the situation and could be the one to control it. "If that is the case, and there is much in this account to imply that it is, we should begin to curtail any and all relations with her."

"I need a bathroom break and so do the dogs." Milla announced this as she stood up. "I don't know what you're talking about that convinces you that Anna Dare is crazy, but I guess I haven't heard it yet." She went down the hallway leaving them alone. Ryan moved over next to Yates to speak softly and still be heard.

"Does she know everything?" He used his attorney-client privilege voice to indicate that he was serious.

"No one knows everything. Except me." Yates was quite proud of himself for getting to make that statement in just that way. When he saw the real look of concern on Ryan's face, he patted his arm. "Not to worry, my boy. I still have a good many, many wild cards that will keep the wolves at bay."

"OK." Reading aloud for so long had made Ryan a little slaphappy, and he almost laughed at the mixed metaphor that the 12th richest man in the world had just used. Although he managed to keep a straight face, he wondered whether that mistake might be a metaphor for all that was happening, used as it was by a man who believed that no rules of any kind apply to him.

"Outside my boys." Milla returned with the dogs who docilely trotted through the room on their way to the absurdly large pet door cut into the wall. She stood at the window watching and checking her phone. When she decided they should come in, Milla put two fingers in her mouth and emitted a shrill whistle. For a moment, Ryan thought that she had used some sort of instrument to make the sound, but she had not. The dogs crashed through the door, and she directed them back into the other section of the house.

"Is anyone hungry? The kitchen staff is still here." She said this primarily to Yates.

"That sounds like a good idea. Tell them to make up some plates of grilled chicken and stir-fried vegetables." He looked at Ryan who just nodded that he was fine with it. "And maybe some quinoa and guacamole if they have the right avocados."

"They have everything you want." She texted the order.

"Let's start up again and get through this thing." Yates was adamant. "Maybe you should skip the explicit sex parts if there are any more. I mean, I know men who have made love to the most beautiful women in the world and would never say a word about it."

"Nothing should be skipped." Milla had returned to her place on the couch. Yates smiled at her.

"Well, by all means then, read every smutty word."

Chapter 16

BEN FORD

"You clean Anna Dare's house? You know her?" We were in the car pulling out of the motel parking lot. I had waited so long to ask because the news had stunned what was left of my thinking process for a full minute. On top of finding the object, which I never thought we would, and learning that my parents were somehow involved, this additional fact was too much.

"Yup. She is one of my clients. Just like your uncle."

"I guess." She could tell that I was not happy that she had kept that from me.

"Listen. One of the conditions for working there is that I can't tell anybody I work there." She put her hand on my thigh. "There are reporters and all kinds of devious people who want to know anything about Anna."

"But you just told me."

"Yes, I did." She squeezed my thigh. "But you already know some shit nobody else knows, and you don't care if Anna shaves her legs."

"Does she?"

"She has them waxed. She has it all waxed." We both laughed at that, and I let the subject drop.

We ate dinner in a casual little restaurant that, in fact, had a good view of the Mississippi. The people were friendly, the food was good and filling, a steamboat left from the pier with waving passengers and even a calliope. All of that was nice, but was just background for me. Nicki was all I could think about as she shot me her smile or just stood close by my side. Her look created a minor stir in some of boys at the bar, but even their headshakes and thinly disguised leers only added to the pride I felt to be with her. I had the distinct notion that all of the people there could sense that we had something, or had done something special that was about to make our fortune.

"A glass of the top Pinot Noir there will be fine." Nicki said this pointing at the small wine list, and I must have made a face of some kind. As soon as the waitress left, she punched my arm. "What's up with you, player?"

"I'm just amazed by the number of voices you have at your command. Just then, you sounded like my old English teacher in high school."

"You ain't never been with a black girl or even a swirl like me, have you?"

"Swirl?"

"Yeah. I'm only half black or maybe less. Hard to tell in this mixed up country we got." She laughed and took my hand. "We got a way of talkin' for every situation under the sun, every place we have to be." She leaned close and whispered. "You only hear my real voice when we get deep into it."

Nicki did have a thing about talking during sex that I had never encountered before. It made me wonder whether I should speak out more, just to be in the moment as she was. Being in the moment, I kissed her just then without caring that people could be put off by such a public display. The restaurant, as I said, was very casual with a stone floor and distressed wooden tables, but at that moment, it was the best place on earth, bathed in a pure light. The waitress smiled at our entwined hands as she set down our drinks, and I decided to propose a toast to our passion for us to drink to, but she beat me to it.

"Mo money." Noticing that I had held up my glass, she touched hers to mine and offered her own toast as she patted the tote bag on the table. I don't remember whether I had told her yet that I would absolutely split whatever we got for my parent's notebook, but I guessed she knew that. I wanted to give her everything. Just as I was about to say exactly that, no matter how it sounded, her phone rang. She looked at the number before giving me a wink and answering it. I supposed it was Anna Dare, but the voice on the other end was male.

"Oh. You answering Miss Anna's texts now?" She made a face. "Uh-huh. I knew something about that, but I never knew nobody could have a phone. No. Thanks, but I'd rather talk to her about spiritual things." She was talking in a low voice, but the waitress, seeing her on the phone, made a U-turn instead of coming to take our order. "No, that will be fine. Good-bye."

"Who was that?"

"That was Dr. Steven Yates, professor of bullshit something or other." I gave her a look of confusion.

"He's Anna Dare's right hand man. Somebody she knew from back in the day, though nobody is sure what day that was. All I know is that he was a professor at Wash U. before she started talking to God and hit the lottery. Ever since then he's been handling all her business affairs and all the money as far as I can tell."

"You didn't want to talk to him? I mean if he has the control of the money, maybe he would just want to take care of it."

"No, I didn't want to talk to him." There was a little delay in the conversation while the waitress took our order. "That man seems to have a problem with Anna giving out her cell number to just some maid." She laughed at that and took a drink. "Thing is, when I am with Miss Dare, we kick our shoes off and talk like there ain't no distance between us at all. Maybe it's because she is sort of a swirl, a real light one, but maybe it's something more than that. I can't explain it." It seems funny now, but I made yet another mental note to never in any way disparage Anna Dare to her, whatever I usually thought about cults. Nicki was as true a believer as the woman who had sold me the tote bag.

"So when will she be available, I wonder?"

"Not today anytime for sure. Maybe not all week. She gone off to this gathering of billionaires out in the woods somewhere in California. That's the kind of thing old Yates likes her to do, meeting with all the rich and powerful people instead of us at the bottom."

"You're not at the bottom of anything. You're the queen of the world." I felt the emotion of saying that and enjoyed watching each word roll over her.

"Don't talk so pretty, boy. I need to eat nice and slow, so I can digest my dinner and have you rough and fast."

"To indigestion." I raised my glass again.

"To anticipation." She clinked my glass. "You want to know the first thing Anna Dare said to me that got to me?"

"What?"

"I knew about the Powerball. Everybody knew about that, and I knew there were four things she said you had to live your life around. If I didn't, some artist painted the words 'Kindness, Pleasure, Learning, and Accomplishment' on each of her bedroom walls. So, I just asked her if somebody like me, who was never going to accomplish or learn much of anything deep, would just be left out of her new thing."

"You just asked her that?"

"Yeah, I did. And she came over and hugged me and said, 'This

God raises everyone up. The worst person in the world can decide to embrace the Way, no matter what they have done before. The Way is always open for everyone to embrace."

"Wow. That must have been something." Again, I was still very skeptical at that time, but I could see how it had affected her.

"She changed my life. Ever since, every act of kindness, any small job I do right, just one new thing I learn how to do, makes me feel that I am doing what God wants me to." Our food arrived. "Maybe your momma and daddy found that God first."

"Didn't I hear you say that pleasure was just as important as the other three?" She nodded and winked but waited to speak until our server left the table.

"Eat up."

We did eat, I'm sure, though I have no memory of what I had. Although I was mildly disappointed that we couldn't unload the note-book before someone tried to take it away from us, nothing could dampen my spirits. I asked if she wanted to take a stroll along the river after dinner, but, as I had hoped, she shook her head. Back at the mo-tel, Nicki again laid the gun on top of the nightstand before pulling the sundress over her head.

"I don't know about you, but that makes me even hotter."

The presence of the gun did not increase my desire for her since it was already at the maximum. For years, I had considered myself some-where in the average range in the bedroom. Women were often pleased, but seldom ecstatic. Until now. Maybe it was her non-stop urging, almost imploring voice that spurred me to heights I had never experi-enced. Or maybe she just made me want to be more than I was for her.

"I love you." I said it that night feeling instantly stupid for doing so. I kissed her immediately to prevent her from feeling any obligation to respond in kind. I was so crazy that I did not care what was really happening. When we were driving to Steele, I mentioned my surprise that she had no tattoos, not even the tiniest heart on her hip. She said something about hating needles, but threw in the fact that she usually got her lover's name inked on her forearm in henna. I got the point about the impermanence, of course, and though I tried to keep it in mind, I really didn't care one bit about the future.

Chapter 17

BEN FORD

I woke up early the next morning, but not as early as Nicki who was already doing some crazy exercise routine in what light managed to leak through the curtains into the room. She wore only a running bra as she balanced effortlessly while skipping an invisible rope. Her hands were held close to her face until they shot out alternately in quick jabs before returning to their position. She did this for a while before dropping to the floor for push-ups; I stopped counting at fifty.

"I guess you didn't get enough exercise last night." She laughed and came up on her knees reaching above her head in a stretch that she held a long time.

"Girl gotta stay fit for action." I was wondering whether that was the sort of thing they said in the Seals when I rolled off the bed and did some push-ups of my own, not counting them either. I collapsed onto the smelly carpet and flipped onto my back. In a flash, she shot across the room to straddle my chest.

"I got something working while you were dreaming your life away. Maybe we can get to Anna Dare sooner instead of later."

"How? She's still in California, right?" I was enjoying the pressure of her bottomless beauty on my chest. She knew it too.

"There's this reporter named Jill Devereaux who did the only interview Anna ever gave to anybody."

"I know. I have a copy of it." She nodded, and I remembered that she had looked through my backpack.

"Yeah, well, Anna really has a thing for this Jill. She always takes her calls no matter what is going on. I've seen her do it."

"Did she know her before she became famous?"

"Don't know. But I been texting with Jill this morning already, and her nose for news smells something. She wants to see us tonight."

"You know her?" She seemed hurt that I would ask that question.

"Yeah, I met her while she was doing that interview. I thought she would be all snooty cause I think she's from old St. Louis money and all that shit. She all right, but kind of crazy in a rich girl kind of way." She moved her face close to me, and I kissed her. "So what's you think about that for a plan?"

"Ok. It would be great if we could make some money. Because in that email Anna Dare didn't seem to want to pay for it."

"Hard to say from that if she knew what he really had." She thought a second. "It's hard to say what it really means."

"Do you think this Jill would pay for it?"

"I didn't tell her exactly what it is. Just that we had something important to Anna."

"You think she will go for that?"

"She is pretty crazy about Anna too. She won't do anything to hurt her I don't think." She held my arms down firmly perpendicular to my body while she slid slowly down my trunk until we were face to face. She was sweaty from her workout, but I didn't care about that or anything.

We drove back from Cape on what I remember was a perfect spring day, with the urging of nature reflected in every darting bird, each nervous rabbit looking to cross the highway, all the scraggly weeds trying to flourish for a few hours in a ditch. The dodge devoured the road with monstrous growls while I read my parent's notebook. From time to time, I compared it to a copy of *The Way* that I bought at a truck stop where we got gas. The old clerk who took my money told me it had changed his life forever.

In several chapters, I found that the book had been copied word for word, and other times there were only minor changes. The main difference was in the beginning of the notebook in which my parents were writing about taking a motorcycle trip (it was heartbreaking to read how much they loved riding together considering how they died) to some place in Iowa and had a spiritual revelation by the campfire. It seems that they both heard a voice at the same time speak the words "kindness, learning, pleasure, accomplishment." They didn't know what to think or quite believe what happened, and my father searched around for somebody playing a trick in the woods. The words had such a strange effect on them that they came home and wrote about the thoughts that had also come to them on the ride home or as my mother wrote, they "let a strange force move the pen in our hands."

"Pretty amazing, isn't it?" With her eyes plastered to the road, Nicki might have been talking about anything, but I knew what she meant. "Those are your parents with all your genes floating around in them, the ones who wrote the book that is changing the world. What you think about that?"

"It seems impossible." At that time I was still torn in my feelings about my parents being so ready to believe in something like this, even if it was a big deal. They had never said anything to me about it, and we never went to church or anything, which may be the point.

"Maybe nobody will believe it, but you know it's true."

"I am not sure what is true, though. Did she get a copy from my parents or my uncle? My uncle might have known her a long time ago."

"Or…" she hesitated. "What if your parents and Anna just happened to have the exact same revelation at a different time that caused them to write down the exact same words? Wouldn't that freak everybody to hell and back?"

"It would." Just that morning I had seen on the web that some Catholic Bishops were starting to look into whether Anna Dare's visions could be considered miraculous along the lines of Medjugorje. Even the Pope expressed an interest in meeting her and there was talk of her going to Rome. Somewhere after a rest stop, I found the Jill Devereaux interview and read it. I have, for many reasons, read the whole thing several times during my isolation here. That day I read a part that resonated deep into my core, especially as Nicki drove **silently beside me.**

JD: Some people have complained that your book, your newer testament as you call it, spends almost no time discussing the importance of love in your vision of God."

AD: My book does not address many things. I don't talk at all about hair-care products.

JD: But, seriously, love is so important. For many it is the reason for living at all.

AD: I think of it like health. If you live a certain way, exercise and eat right and so forth, health will usually come to you. If you are kind and learned and accomplished and open to pleasure, love will likely come your way.

JD: That word "likely" may be a problem for some people who look to see you as one of God's prophets.

AD: If they want guarantees, they are with the wrong prophet.

The Way is simply the right course to take no matter what happens. They will know that as soon as they live it.
JD: So we should not think of love as important?
AD: Love is a wonderful thing to have in your life. But you must always remember that the only control you have in love is the amount you give; what you receive in return is beyond your control. That is true in romantic love, familial love, love of your fellow humans. If you live in accordance with the way of God, any return at all will be the sweetest icing on the delicious cake you eat every day.

Chapter 18

BEN FORD

The Prophet is with us Right Now. This is Anna Dare Country.
A billboard announced this as we entered St. Louis County on Highway 44. The County is a collection of many, many cities, not one of which is the actual city of Saint Louis. Some of these cities are comically small in both area and population, their names announced on the side of the highway on signs that are meaningless to the big world. As I mentioned, most of the residents of these towns consider themselves from Saint Louis and, I suppose, can justify that from the name of their county. There is a local understanding about the connotations of living in Ferguson or Clayton or Beverly Hills (they have one), but now as an outsider I thought it all silly since it was the same melting pot. All would claim some great pop star or sports hero as their own.

"I need to stop by my place and find something to wear. This Jill puts on the dog in the clothes department, so I can't be looking like a beast next to her." I ran a finger across the crotch of her jeans to reassure her, but also to remind myself that was a thing I could actually do in the new world I was living in.

"You think I should check over at my uncle's house? See what's going on?"

"You sold that house, big man." She tapped my thigh. "No reason to be going over there at all. We already got what everybody's looking for." I wasn't exactly sure who "everybody" might be, but I didn't really care. There was love and money in the air. Although I had most of what I ever wanted if I didn't do anything with the notebook, I was not immune to wanting more from a ridiculously rich woman like Anna Dare.

"Maybe I should ask them what they'd pay for the thing if they are still over there."

"You ever think that they were hooked up with the guys who jumped us at the hotel?"

I had not that at the time because I had not really been thinking straight for a few day or really thinking about anything except Nicki and all the actual and potential money floating into my life. If I could have had three wishes, those would have been the first two; I would not even have considered a third.

"So where does this well-dressed Jill live, anyway? In the City?" I was picturing her in Soulard or on the South Side because she was young, associated with money, and wrote for the Riverfront Times.

"Nope. She a North County girl now, though she don't own up to it too much. She has a great house, though."

In twenty minutes, we were back in Ferguson stopped at a red light next to a local police car. Nicki waved, and they waved back. Her house had a small garage in back, but she did not park in it leaving her car in the driveway. There was still a van parked in my uncle's driveway. After looking at the bay window for a full minute, she went up the steps to unlock the front door, immediately turning off the alarm system on a pad just inside the small living room. Entering just behind her, I thought it was the sparest house I had ever been in where a woman lived. There were no pictures on the walls and the only furniture in the front room was a leather couch and a coffee table that had only a TV remote on it. The flat screen sat on a bare metal stand.

"Home, sweet, home." Nicki said this and walked quickly through each of the four small rooms. When she returned, I was sitting on the couch considering turning on the TV until she began to say something about needing a hot shower or "something hot." She undressed right there in the living room.

I pulled her next to me, the backs of her now naked thighs making a squeak as she slid across the leather. My hunger for her had not abated one bit, and I treated her like a queen, my tongue flicking everywhere as I held her hands in mine. In her husky voice, she gave directions; I followed them for a long time. When she pulled my t-shirt over my head to bite my chest, I said another stupid thing.

"I don't care what happens next. You've made my life a thing worth having." Looking back on that statement, I might have seemed pathetic. I also must have said something I had been thinking about in the car about even being OK with her eventually moving on. I went on like that for a while before she kissed me to shut me up. She was laughing when we broke it off.

"Boy, you crazy. I said I ain't good being owned outright by nobody, and that's why you'll kick me to the curb when you get tired of it, but I'll never lose it for you. I mean that." I started to react to her words, but she put a hand over my mouth. While I just looked at her, she turned around with her knees on the cushions and opened the curtain that was in front of her face. "Listen. I want you to stop talking and do me right now while I'm looking out at the street. I stare out just this way all the time, and now every time I do, I will be thinking of you."

It was easy to comply with her request as she went on to say some things that I had always wanted to hear in just the way I wanted to hear them, though I never knew it before that moment, the substance being beyond my imagination. I said a few things myself and the moment filled with sweet hyperbole as I wished I could break every second into a million pieces and live them one at a time forever. When I was spent, she continued to grip me with some internal muscles until reality slowly entered the room with its ticking clock. Her cell phone, on the floor in front of the couch, also rang, and she answered it.

"Hey! I need to borrow a car to go someplace tonight." While she was listening to the answer, she flicked a drop of semen from my penis with her tongue. "Yeah, that would be perfect. Any time before six. See you then." She ended the call and hugged me.

"What's wrong with your car?"

"Nothing, but too many people seen it around lately. Best for us to take a new ride out to Jilly's house."

I didn't say anything, just held her clinging to the moment. I adored everything about her almost without caring how she felt about me. I suppose that none of this is pertinent to what the Great World cares about, and I am certain that no one will ever read it. Still, I imagine Nicki reading it, her dark eyes rolling slowly over each word as they try to reproduce that moment in time when we were happy just to hold each other in that house in Ferguson as if Time did not exist. She may not remember it this way, but at least she will know the divine weight of the longing I experienced that day.

Chapter 19

BEN FORD

At some point Nicki took her shower after giving me strict instructions to answer the door for no one after she reset the alarm. While she was in the bathroom, I took the briefest tour of the house. Her bedroom was as spare as the living room with only a double bed perfectly made and some sort of Ikea dresser. The other bedroom had only a folding chair with a laptop next to it. The kitchen was immaculate, but there was no food in the refrigerator, just some bottled water and energy drinks. The pantry had only two boxes of some protein bars I had never heard of. I asked her if I could have one, and she said I could in a way that suggested I didn't have to ask.

Back in the living room, I read some more of the notebook easily locating the corresponding pages in Anna Dare's bestseller. As I digested the somewhat complicated explanations of how to live a life according to The Way, I began to have some complicated feelings of my own. On the one hand, I was starting to believe that someone gave Anna Dare a copy of this to read many years ago and she saved it until she won the lottery, especially the second time, when she felt that some higher power had chosen her for something. This meant that she had lied about having the experience herself and was a fraud. On the other hand, I was not comfortable with my own parents being the authors of something as strange as what I had read, thinking that some voices had come to them the way they did to the crazy preachers on TV. On yet another hand, there was great power in their words and a depth of belief that affected me. My mother's poems were collected in the Anna Dare book under the heading "New Psalms." In a particular one, her voice was so clear that the sound of it was almost in the room.

God is never far from you
Though some days hard to see.
Your dear eyes can be fogged.
By sloth.
By cruelty.
By an apathy for wisdom.
And most of all by the despair that finds no bread of Life.
Remove those clouds.
The light will fall upon you, as does the warmth of the sun
Requiring no faith to feel it.

"You getting down with Anna, now? Or at least your moms and pop?" Nicki emerged wearing only a towel wrapped around her head and pointing to the book in my hand. I could not tell whether she was the sort of person who was so proud of her body that she loved to show it off at any opportunity or was just absolutely comfortable with herself. I was truly happy with either explanation, but I tried to be cool with her nakedness as difficult as it was.

"I wonder if we will ever find out the whole story of how this happened. Anna Dare might just buy it and send us packing with no explanation." I adored every single cell of her that was on display in front of me as I spoke. My nonchalance was not particularly convincing.

"Maybe, but I have this feeling we will find out something pretty soon." She held up the remote. "You want to watch TV while I finish fixing myself up?"

I nodded, and she turned the flat screen on before handing me the remote and heading back into the bathroom. Alone, I scrolled aimlessly through the middle of chase scenes and laugh tracks until I came across a talk show on a news channel that was discussing Anna Dare. As on most of these programs, everyone was too angry for my taste, but I listened for a minute.

"She may be your prophet, but she is not mine." Some old guy in a bowtie said this trying, unsuccessfully, to control his emotions.

"She is your prophet, my friend, but you are free to accept or reject her." A much younger woman said this very calmly.

"I reject her." Another even older man took a deep breath before continuing. "You might not be aware of it, but this woman may be about to destroy the Judeo-Christian tradition in a single generation if she is not stopped." The young woman, no longer calm, put up a hand to silence him.

"I know that you find it difficult to accept a woman as the prophet of God, but many people see her as just that, people who find your attempts to silence her laughable." What followed was the sort of yelling that makes me seldom watch such programs. I turned it off and picked up the Jill Devereaux interview with Anna Dare. I thought I should read the whole thing before we saw her that night. There is a part where the discussion drifted into politics that I found especially interesting.

JD: Are you a liberal or a conservative?
AD: I hate those labels. All politicians in America, whether they admit it or not, follow The Way. Although they make very human mistakes, like Jim Crow or putting

> *Japanese-Americans in camps, they eventually see their errors and work to correct them.*
>
> *JD: I am shocked that you find such consensus in our politics, especially now.*
>
> *AD: You have to know how to look at things. We have this great document, The Constitution that was the beginning of the realization of the Way of God. Imagine the audacity of allowing absolute freedom of speech while rejecting cruel and unusual punishments.*
>
> *JD: So you believe the Founding Fathers were secret followers of The Way?*
>
> *AD: I do. If they had truly been devout Puritans or Quakers or Anglicans, the document would have been much different. The Declaration, also, would never have been able to imagine a nation founded on Life, Liberty and the Pursuit of Happiness without the God of the Way influencing it.*

As I was reading this there was a loud knock on the front door, the sort of knock the police use to make sure you can't ignore it. Nicki appeared wearing a purple robe moving sideways through the living room. Both of her hands were clasped tightly around a pistol, but it was different from the one she had been using. I was almost certain of it. Instead of going to the door, she peeped through the front window keeping the gun pointed up. Kneeling on the couch, she was in almost the same position as before and only slightly more dangerous. When she exhaled, I knew there was no danger.

"I hear you knockin'!" Nicki said this as she jumped off the couch. She opened the door quickly allowing a tall, very solid looking man wearing a leather jacket that seemed too heavy for spring to enter. He did not remove his very expensive sunglasses or advance past the foyer. He and Nicki exchanged a sort of fist bump in which both of then pulled away immediately upon contact as if they changed their minds. She introduced us; he nodded in my direction.

"I hear you all need a loaner." He sort of said this to me as he took out his car keys though it was hard to tell who he was looking at, and Nicki answered.

"Just a trade for a few nights. You can take my car if you promise to only drive 20 miles over the speed limit." She picked up her keys from the floor, and exchanged them with his.

"I'll be real gentle with it after I see if it still gives me a thrill." He said this without any emotion, but I started wondering whether this Max was one of Nicki's old boyfriends, one that she had refused to belong to. He seemed like the type who would have a problem with that arrangement, and I wondered (and still wonder) if I would be any different. I was glad that he left almost immediately, gunning the engine of the Challenger as he tore down the street. Nicki cursed after him, but she was not angry. She shook her phone at me before I could say anything.

"Just got a text from Jill. She wants us to come in time for sunset, so we need to get on the double. You want to grab a shower?" She seemed different since Max had been there, but I couldn't quite put my finger on it or didn't want to.

I took a quick shower and shaved in her tiny bathroom, amazed by how my life had changed, wondering if it was for the better or worse. I put on the same jeans and my last clean shirt just as Nicki opened the door to reveal a red leather outfit that came straight from my id. She laughed at the look on my face.

"Girl's got to get her slut on once and a while, especially around this Jill, or a man forgets what he can have." A part of me wanted to forget the whole adventure part of Nicki and me, forget about the notebook and Jill Devereaux and even Anna Dare, but I could tell somehow all of this went together. I was just hoping that after it was resolved there would be some sort of life left for us, even if it would not ever be completely normal.

Chapter 20

BEN FORD

The vehicle that Max had left us was a very sturdy black Escalade, another model of car I had never been in. Nicki drove well within the speed limit as we pulled up onto Highway 270 headed east, her eyes again darting around constantly. With the tote bag on the floor in front of my feet and my new love at the wheel, I felt lucky. Although I wasn't sure that it was a good idea to tell a reporter our little secret, I trusted Nicki that it would put us closer to a big payday. Besides that, I was just enjoying the ride.

I had read online that this Jill had been born and raised in the wealthy Saint Louis suburb of Ladue and changed her name from Corrine Ambrose for some reason, probably to aggravate her rich parents. One big criticism of her was that she was not much of a real journalist with haters citing some of her freelance articles in *Saint Louis Magazine* about where to grab the top 10 best burgers locally or great bars to go to on Tinder first dates. Even the early articles she wrote for *The Riverfront Times* seemed lightweight before she got the big interview. Also, Anna Dare picked her through the strange process of just selecting her name from the list of people who asked to interview her by some divine guidance. Jill, of course, became a star, not just locally, but as a guest on numerous shows herself as the only reporter who actually had access to the new prophet.

"So where does she live?" We were still going east on 270 having passed any turns that would have taken us to the swankier parts of town where I assumed she lived.

"You'll be surprised. I was when she took me there."

"So you guys are close friends?"

"I wouldn't say that exactly." She waited while an Acura SUV slowly passed us. "Like I said, I met her while I was cleaning at Anna's, and she was coming over for the interview. Anna always wanting everybody to know everybody else, so we met and clicked."

"But you have been to her apartment?"

"House. Yeah, we went out for drinks to celebrate after she wrapped things up with Anna. She knew she was going to be hot shit, and got so plastered that I had to drive her home. She's really proud of the place, but she ain't no snob about it. Maybe that's why Anna picked her."

I was going to say that I had read that Anna had never met her before the interview, but I decided to not go there because most of the stuff on the internet is crap. I was finding it hard to believe that this Jill had a cool house as we continued east. For a year, I had dated a woman who lived in Illinois, near Alton, so I had driven this same route many times always dreading that I might have a flat tire or something in this part of the county where the surrounding communities are poorer and more inclined to crimes of all kinds. The farther east we went, the more I imagined that we would soon cross the Mississippi. We didn't, and at Riverview she put on her signal to exit.

"Really?"

"Hang on!" We turned north after the exit as the road plunged into some heavy woods. For one brief second it crossed my mind that there might not be a house or a Jill Devereaux down any of the country lanes, places that seemed perfect for dumping a body. The houses that did appear in the failing light were old and not particularly interesting. I suppose my doubts were still nagging at me (even down here, writing this, they still nag me. Sorry, Nicki.) I actually stiffened up expecting the world to return to what it had usually been for me when we turned onto a short road blocked by a black gate. We stopped in front of a keypad as Nicki typed in the code.

"Open Sesame." She said that as the piece of wrought iron slowly cranked open to clear the path for us. In one turn, we were on a gravel road as large houses now loomed slowly into view. When she pulled into a circle drive and stopped next to a BMW, I figured we had arrived. We took a narrow walkway that led from the circle through some tall, thick bushes to a little courtyard where a very unusual house, one story, but with two wings that merged in a sharp right angle, stood with a light blazing in every window. It was made of a white stone that seemed much more exotic than the stucco I assumed from a distance. The front door was in the center of the 90-degree angle, and a woman stood at the opening holding a martini glass: Jill Devereaux. She wore a black outfit that looked like pajamas and seemed to strike a pose with one hand on her hip as we walked toward her.

"Welcome to my humble abode. So glad you arrived before I got totally crunk on my own." Her hair was a dark auburn tied in a very thick ponytail. When Nicki introduced us, she pinched my palm with two fingers instead of shaking my hand. Nicki got a long hug and a kiss on both cheeks. Jill asked us what we were drinking.

"Slow down, girl. We're not up here to party." Nicki said this very seriously until she broke into a crazy laugh. "Gimme a damn drink." Jill extended her arm with a flourish directing us to precede her into the house. When I passed close to her, I noticed that for a redhead she was entirely devoid of freckles, and I wondered if she'd had them removed as rich girls do because they can do anything.

The corridor we entered was covered with light brown paneling, which the hardwood floors matched perfectly. The huge den we came to that must have been one leg of the right angle was also completely encased in the same wood, and featured furniture that was geometric and modern and seemed seldom sat upon. Jill offered me a seat on the very large couch that was stiff, but I guess retro or something. There was an afghan on one end that had the word "pleasure" woven into it; I assumed the other three words were there as well. After getting me a beer and Nicki a martini, Jill lowered herself onto a red leather chaise, her white feet with their pale pink toenails looking more like works of art than physical appendages. She reached behind her and pushed a button on the wall, and the curtains at the picture window slid slowly open revealing the vast gray expanse of the Mississippi below us. I must have gasped my surprise sufficiently.

"Forgive me, but I love doing that when people come over. This is the best view in Saint Louis, and nobody even knows these houses are up here, thank God." It was spectacular especially as the light gently played across the great river.

"The Mississippi is really something." I think I said something dumb like that, not quite having found my bearings between the house and Jill's voice that had a strange musical quality, classical, but still music.

"We are actually at the confluence of the wide Missouri and the mighty Mississippi." She drained her drink and seemed to consider whether I knew what "confluence" meant or maybe just consider me generally. She pointed at Nicki. "So you are seeing this little wild thing in a romantic, making the beast with two backs, sort of way?" She tapped my knee. "Well, good luck with that. She drank me well under the table on our one and only night out."

"We were both under the table if I remember."

"I was much further under than you since you were still able to drive your little muscle car while I kept hitting my head on the dashboard." She turned to me. "She could have easily taken advantage of me."

"I did."

"Damn and I missed it." She looked at her glass again. "Now what is this exciting thing you want to reveal to your roving reporter?" She put a hand on my knee, but she was looking at Nicki.

I took the initiative and explained that my uncle had left me a document that my parents had written in the 90s (I left out Miss Dixon). Jill smiled politely until I dropped the big bomb as it related to Anna Dare. She had just retrieved her glass from the little table and was snaking her tongue inside to access the remaining drop of the martini when her dark blue eyes opened very wide.

"Did you bring it with you? I want to see it." She sat up now. Nicki had removed the notebook from the tote bag and tapped it suggestively.

"You can look, but you got to promise not to say nothing to nobody until we all agree on what's best for my boy Ben here. He'd like to make some money." Jill gave a fake look of being shocked.

"Of course, of course. Discretion is always the better part of everything." She pinched my knee. Nicki handed her the notebook and turned to me.

"I think we can trust her as far as we can throw her, and that's pretty far." She stood up. "You want another martini?"

"I do, you bad influence." Jill slid next to me on the couch handling my parents' notebook as if it might be radioactive. She even sniffed it and bent the pages testing the age of it, I guess. She speed read the first section, then turned to me speaking in a whisper. "Are you in the anti-Dare camp, young fellow?" Jill was a few years younger than I was, but she seemed much older.

"No. I am just trying to understand how all this happened." I whispered also, which seemed very intimate.

"And get paid." She said this without judgement, and I thought she might be ready to write me a check for it right then. She went back to reading. "Nicki told me that your parents are dead, so the only one who could maybe explain this is Anna Dare. I will tell you that I believe in her message, but she has some 'splainin' to do."

"I think she knows about it." I mentioned the email she sent to my uncle. "I probably just need to talk to her if you can make that happen. Then we can find out if this is a thing at all."

"Oh, it's a thing, Big Ben. It's very much a thing." Nicki came back with two drinks.

"What you think, you hot shot celebrity reporter always on television every time I turn it on?" She handed Jill a martini and sat on the other side of me.

"I don't know. It could be some elaborate fake, but something in my gut tells me it isn't." She took a healthy swig. "You know, there has been a rumor on the internet for some time that someone else wrote *The Way*, and that Anna just preaches it. A reporter for the *Post* met a guy in a parking garage a couple months ago who told him that he had proof that Steven Yates wrote the whole thing, but found a way to make it mysteriously appear on Anna's computer in such a way that she could think it was put there by God, Himself. He turned out to have no credible evidence, but this kind of thing would surely give credence to all of those rumors if it ever got out." Nicki plucked the notebook from the reporter's hands.

"It sure might hurt book sales some." Jill shook her head fiercely, her ponytail brushing the side of my face.

"Who cares about that? Anna almost gives the book away for free." She was worked up now. "The religious community is trying to find some way to get ahead of this story of the only prophet in town. The

Catholics want to declare her whatever the fuck they declare somebody who has divine revelations, and every other religion wants her on their team unless they can expose her as a charlatan." She tapped the notebook. "People believe in her words. If she got them somewhere else, it's a very big deal." I couldn't tell if she was more excited about breaking the story or squashing it, but she was excited.

"So call her." Nicki ate one of the olives in her martini. "She always takes your calls, I hear. Let's just see if she cares one way or the other and go from there."

"I could certainly do that. I could say that the woman who cleans your house and her boyfriend have a hand-written copy of your book that they think they can blackmail you with, but wouldn't that make me an accomplice or something?" She stretched her arms above her head briefly exposing the flesh at the bottom of her spine.

"You could say you were doing her a solid by bringing us to her before anybody else gets ahold of it. She wants this thing." Nicki leaned across me to be closer to Jill's face. "And a bunch of other people want it." She told her about the guy trying to kidnap me at the hotel leaving out the part that she had rescued me.

"Yeah, things are getting crazy violent now with the Twitter trolls. They are actually leaving their basements since they can't get to Anna, because she never engages on social media, just shows up at Jack in the Box and buys everybody lunch. I'm glad nobody knows I live up here because my death threats are increasing geometrically." I decided I should say something.

"So you don't want to help us? Maybe I'll just start hanging out at Jack in the Box." I acted as if I was about to get up and leave. Jill grabbed my forearm.

"Wait a minute. I'll make you a deal, hunky-boy. Whatever Anna tells you about this thing, you tell me, word for word. I won't do anything with the information as far as writing about you, but I want to know. Deal?"

I nodded wondering if I liked being called "hunky-boy" or not. When she kissed my cheek to seal the deal, she made a loud cartoon smooch noise, and I could tell she left some of her dark brown lipstick on my face. Picking up her cell phone from the table, she strode into the other leg of the right angle of the house before placing her call.

"You think we can trust her." Nicki and I, alone now on someone else's couch waiting to hear news, seemed like a real couple. At least I felt that way.

"Trust, but verify." She kissed me on the other cheek gently. "We'll know in a hot minute or two what kind of juice she has."

"At least it's a cool view." We walked together to the picture window. A barge drifted by, just barely visible now in the middle of the river. It was almost out of sight when Jill came back in the room almost at a run.

"Sweet sleeping Jesus!" She said that with a sort of black accent, and I looked at Nicki to see if she was upset. She laughed. "Anna almost came through the phone having some sort of vision about seeing you or something. She's cancelling golf or swimming naked with billionaires to be here tomorrow night."

"You didn't have to go through Yates, then?"

"For about five seconds until I told him it was me, and it was life and death." She was pretty proud of herself.

"Where does she want to meet?" I was trying to act as if I took meetings with famous people every day. Jill came over and hugged me.

"Ferguson, Missouri, you lucky guy. You get to see her house and hang out with the woman who talks to God." She did not let go.

"OK. Did she say what time?"

"Around nine, but she said she would call you. Dress casual because she surly will." She hugged me tighter. "Don't forget we have a deal."

"Scout's honor, though I washed out of the scouts." It was a strange moment with her still holding on to me. Jill is very attractive, but with her easy manner, she seemed more like someone I had known since grade school who could still charm me in a childish way.

"We'll give you the whole story, girl, but it surprises me that Anna doesn't just tell you herself." Nicki pulled on her shoulder gently until she released me.

"I know. It's a conundrum, it is." She went over to a very modern black lacquer desk in the corner and came back with a small recording device. "I know there is not much difference between a reporter and a whore, but put a little something on the dresser before you leave me."

The something was to make me recap my life with special emphasis on my parents, exactly how they died, anything I could remember, especially anything that could tie them to Anna. Because she was from Saint Louis, Jill wanted to know where they went to high school, and she whistled when I told her my mom went to Nerinx Hall, a Catholic school. She showed me an old picture of Anna Dare and asked if I remembered ever seeing her when I was a kid. I didn't. She loved the fact that many of the psalms in *The Way* had been used as little bedtime stories for me. She took out a copy and asked me to find one of the favorites that I could remember hearing. When I pointed to it, she read it aloud.

You stand right now on the perfect place in the Universe,
Not too hot, nor too cold.
It is a Goldilocks planet
That gives you air, sky, mud
And thoughts and great urges.
You have all the luck there is to have.

"I can't believe this is happening." Jill was pounding the book on her knee very hard. "I really believe you, but you have to understand the implications of your story, this document you have."

"I guess it's a big deal." She made a fake "duh" sound.

"It's the biggest deal there is." She stepped back and spread her arms wide. "I don't know you, Ben, or what you want out of life, but whatever it is, Anna can make it happen. She owns the world, and she seems to want to get to know you. Just try to remember what all is at stake here." Her eyes filled with tears. Nicki tugged at my arm.

"He understands all that shit." Nicki was ready to go. "Take Ben's number and have Miss Dare call when she wants to talk." Jill typed my number into her phone and looked me in the eyes.

"Don't forget about me, Ben. I want to hear the end of this story." She took both of us in her arms in a sort of group hug that did make me feel as if I had all the luck there is, for a second. As we walked back across the little courtyard, the sounds of country filled my ears with all the crickets, an owl, a coyote acknowledging my power.

Chapter 21

BEN FORD

"Well, that went pretty damn chocolate, player." Nicki said this as soon as we shut the car doors. "You get to meet the prophet, which means there is something worth something in this bag."

"She may want me to just give it to her. That's what she told my uncle." As we approached the iron gates, they just opened up. On the other side, Nicki stopped the car.

"I think things have changed with his death maybe." She put her hand on top of mine. "Anna don't want nobody else getting hurt where she might be the cause of it."

"So you think my uncle was killed over this notebook?" I had been trying not to think that, but it had seemed logical for a while.

"Maybe. I don't know. What I do know is that you getting this document to Anna is what he would have wanted and the best thing you could do in your life." She was starting to seem a little too devout again, and I think she could tell I was not responding. "So what you think about that Jill?"

"She's OK."

"You think?" Now I thought I should change the subject as we started back down a dark Riverview Drive back to the highway.

"So let's say Anna Dare, just to settle this thing, decides to lay a million bucks on me for this notebook. Where should we go? Maybe they haven't heard of her in Australia yet." She laughed.

"She's big everywhere. She's big in spite of being trashed by every religious leader, pundit, man of God, mostly men, there is. They all starting to come around now, now that they can feel the earth starting to move beneath them."

I didn't say anything, partly because I was thinking about going back to her house to celebrate and peel that outfit from her and partly because I was wondering whether it would be worse if she was a religious fanatic or just a girl out to make money from the opportunity I presented. I said nothing else just then because a big, black F-150 truck pulled out from one of the country roads right in front of us and stopped. Nicki braked hard hitting the horn as we slid to about five feet from the pick-up. As soon as I realized that the truck was not going anywhere, Nicki slammed the Escalade into reverse only to stop immediately when another truck blocked the road behind us. Two men got out of the front truck, one of them holding a shotgun.

"Put your hands up!" Nicki said that to me as she did the same, her face locked into a hard look. I could feel the blood pounding in my nose, and I was trying to think of something that I should say before they made us open the doors. I couldn't think of anything fast enough. Just as the men were close enough for me to see that they were wearing Halloween masks, the rubber kind that pull over your head, Nicki stomped on the accelerator causing them to jump out of the way, the shotgun exploding across our windshield. It didn't shatter, and we drove as close to the front pick-up as possible, sideswiping it a little to avoid the deep ditch on the side of the road. There were some popping sounds behind us and some metal thumps into the body of our car, but we were back on the road with the digital speedometer flicking through the numbers until we reached 90. Nicki said nothing until we were on the highway.

"You better ask for two million now." She was laughing which could have made me relax, but didn't. I was shook up. "And get her to throw me a little somethin' somethin'."

"So I'm guessing you still don't think we should call the cops?" She shook her head. I kept looking back for one of the pickups or maybe flashing lights coming up fast behind us. I saw neither.

"Yeah, you can tell them that your girlfriend almost ran over some guys who want to take the thing you are fixin' to blackmail Anna Dare with. That would make their shift. No, baby, we don't need the popo."

Of course, of course, I knew by then that Nicki was into something besides housecleaning. I assumed it was drugs, which would explain how she could afford her car, and how she knew someone with a bullet proof Escalade she could borrow (she said Max had bought it at a police auction). If she really had been almost a Navy Seal, that would explain her ease with weapons and violence generally, but her current life was criminal which was why she wanted nothing to do with the cops. I will admit that I began right then to lean more onto not trusting her much to my great shame now as I write this.

We drove around aimlessly it seemed through that spring night going mostly the speed limit until she took the exit for Lambert Airport. For a moment, I thought she might be ready to leave town and worry about the payoff later. She pulled well away from any cars in the back of the upper level of the parking garage. Picking up the tote bag, she took out her phone and got out of the car briefly inspecting the holes in the rear fender.

"What now? New Zealand?" I was standing next to her watching a car come slowly down the row toward us. Nicki slammed her hip into mine to move me out of the aisle. A little girl in the back seat made her doll wave at me.

"We Uber the fuck outta here." She was already pressing the app on her phone as she started walking toward the elevator that would take us down to the pickup level. Her other hand was inside the tote bag as she carried it probably, I supposed, gripping the pistol. She called Max in the elevator to tell him where we were leaving his car, but she offered no explanation although he must have said something funny, the way she smiled. When I started to say something, she kissed me just as the doors opened onto a group of college girls already in high spirits who gave a little cheer.

The Uber driver was about my age with the exhausted look of someone that never gets quite enough sleep working in the gig economy. He took us just across the highway to the Marriott, but we made a U-turn in the lobby and walked to a smaller hotel a half mile away in case anybody was looking for us, which I assumed they were. Checking in, Nicki used her credit card, a card that I noticed had a name other than hers (and a matching driver's license), but it worked. The also tired desk clerk seemed uninterested in whether we were fugitives from the law or international terrorists.

"What a dump!" Nicki said this as soon as we entered the small room that was spare and cheap and not especially clean with a faded stain at the foot of the bed. She double locked the door leaning the single wooden chair underneath the knob in case "somebody get a key." She sat on the bed with a little bounce to test the firmness. "Nothing like a cheap motel after you've had the shit scared out of you to get the juices flowing. You feel me?"

I did. When I joined her on the bed and pulled her to me, I felt the butt of the pistol in the back of her leather pants. I didn't see her move it from the bag. She laughed and set it on the nightstand putting her other hand on my chest to slow down the pace of my ardor. Slowly peeling off her outfit, she started whispering in a way that sounded like some slow blues song.

"You gonna see the prophet tomorrow, big shot, big man, big money. Tonight you gonna find all your religion right here. Yes, yes. It's time to worship at this altar, like Adam did when God wasn't looking. Or you gonna be like Moses and give me some commandments? I'll take them. Or do you want a few of mine?"

It was terrific in a way I had never thought actually existed as she encouraged me, dared me, to ask for things I had not really considered. Nothing surprised her or seemed remotely repugnant as if we were both in some sort of cult together, the kind that drives you mad. I have to say I wanted to be mad with her, wanted to exist only on our plane of reality that encompassed everything in those few square feet of space.

The sad thing about the paragraph above is that it once again made me wonder if I was worthy of such passion when I had never before been worthy of it. I was thinking that all of the business about my parents and my uncle and my sudden wealth probably had disoriented me, the way a lottery winner must feel when the number in his hand matches the one on TV. All the change, all the luck must seem not just too good to be true, but patently untrue, an only temporary state that has to revert to normal at some point. Nicki was in the shower when I saw the text from Jill Devereaux that said. "Nicki is not who she seems. Beware."

I should have said something immediately, but to my great shame, I kept the message to myself. Maybe it all made sense to me. When I think back on that moment, Jill seemed to be telling me the Truth because it fit so perfectly with everything that had ever happened to me. Things that are too good to be true never are or at least never last.

Chapter 22

YATES

"OK, OK. Who the fuck is this Nicki? Why is she doing any of this at all? I don't get it." Ryan did not think that Yates wanted an answer, and even though he had read the entire story, he was not sure that he knew the truth. It was all speculation. Milla seemed not too interested in his response as she looked at her phone.

"We have sustenance." A minute later three women wearing white blouses and black pants appeared carrying silver trays. Milla instructed them where to place the food on a stressed wooden table before inspecting what they had delivered. Satisfied, she dismissed the women who had not said one word during the time they were there. After the silent trio was well gone, Ryan answered Yates' question.

"You have to keep in mind that we have nothing that vouches for the authenticity of this document, and..."

"Yes, we all understand that because you keep saying it." Ryan had not seen him so angry, and Yates, seeing the look on his face, tried to regain control by changing the subject. "My own brother there on the ground in the Show-Me state was supposed to know everything that was going on. Now, he appears to be having a nervous breakdown while

Anna renews her spiritual perfection. It's disheartening and unacceptable." He went over to the little buffet and started picking at the food.

"Please, eat." Milla extended her arm in Ryan's direction, and he stood up waiting until Yates had filled a plate to consider the fare. Although it was delicious, he would have preferred something ridiculously fattening like a cheeseburger to go along with all this reading about the Midwest. After eating what was probably the perfect quantity and variety of vegetables, Milla asked a question.

"Do you think this whole thing is just a plot to blackmail Robert?" Yates did not let him answer.

"Do you have that note from Anna Dare?"

"Yes, but all it says is that you need to see this." Yates asked to see the note that Ryan produced and handed to him. He and Milla stared at it for a while. Yates finished eating and put his plate on the end table.

"I'm still wondering how someone like her would ever know to send it to you, that you could be the person to make sure that I saw it, no matter where in the world I might be." Yates gently sniffed the note. "Have you ever met Anna Dare?"

"No, I haven't actually met her." Ryan had not been a part of the meeting with all of the wealthiest men in the world that Anna had attended. Yates smiled at Milla as he motioned to Ryan to continue reading.

Chapter 23

BEN FORD

The next morning well after eleven we waited a long time in the seedy lobby of the hotel for Enterprise to deliver a rental car to us. I was feeling terrible for not telling Nicki about the text, but also about the text itself that made me think that I had been a fool all along. Even in the crappy surroundings with no makeup on, Nicki made the head of every salesman and hotel employee turn toward her as they passed through. It was so obvious that she should never be with me unless there was something else going on. Jill was right; she was not who she seemed to be. I had been so ready for her to be part of my lucky break that I had ignored everything.

The car that eventually arrived was an Elantra that only a few days earlier would have seemed great as it still sported a vague trace of new car smell and all, but now it was doggy and ordinary compared to the cars I had been in. As the Enterprise guy was handing us the keys, Nicki got a call that she took, so I drove away from the place going slowly down the service road unsure of a destination. It didn't help my suspicions that her responses on the call were all one word with nothing to clue me in as to whom she might be speaking. She was keeping something from me.

"Get up on Highway 70 going east." She broke off her call and set the phone in her lap. "We're going to take a tour of the 'hood." She gave my thigh a squeeze and I complied. I had not texted Jill Devereaux back yet, but I became more and more anxious to do so with every minute. Although Nicki probably thought I was nervous about taking the Goodfellow exit and heading south into the rough part of St. Louis, I had my own secret now and was having trouble holding onto it. At first Goodfellow is not an especially threatening street with a Federal office complex on one side and no dangerous gang types hanging out. After we crossed Natural Bridge Road, there were more and more empty, dilapidated houses. The stares of the young black men on the corners or sitting on the stoops became harder, more questioning of some white guy driving here probably looking for drugs or some other trouble. Nicki waved and smiled at all of them. The side streets we were passing were ones I had only heard on the news as scenes of murders. When she indicated that I turn on one, I hesitated, but went ahead and pulled up in front of a narrow brick row house with steel bars on the front windows. The street was empty and quiet which I did not take as a good sign. It was the quiet that comes from fear and despair.

"Relax, baby. It's daylight. The real badass gangbangers don't come out until dark." Still, I noticed her head was on a swivel all the way on the short walk from the car to the house. A big dog in the neighboring yard started barking like crazy, as we knocked on the front door that also had a steel cage around it. It took a long while for someone to flip the three latches with the barking growing fiercer and louder every second. When the door finally opened, a 300-pound black man wearing a long Rams jersey and no pants stood in the entrance.

"Welcome to Xanadu, a stately pleasure dome for your enjoyment." He gave Nicki a big hug and me a smaller one after we were introduced. His name was Langston Butler, and he found everything to be hilarious.

Nicki kidded him a while about being on a "biscuit and gravy" diet and his lack of pants which made him laugh so hard that he went into a coughing fit, but even my asking him if the car would be all right on the street drew a decent chuckle.

"It's all good, my man. I got a camera on it, and anyway ain't nobody trying to boost a Hyundai around here just now. Nobody likes to scare away the crack customers." He made himself laugh at that, and I looked around the place to see if it was a drug house. I have never actually been in a drug house, but this place was too clean and devoid of any clutter except the large computer with two monitors in the living room. An office chair with an unusual, probably ergonomic design for a big man, and a wicker couch with purple cushions were the only pieces of furniture in the living room. The wood floor looked recently swept and had a shine on it. I heard the stomp of footsteps coming down the stairs behind me followed by a scream that froze me in my tracks.

"Hey, girl! Where you been?" A young Asian woman wearing a green silk robe leapt the last three steps to be on our level and grab Nicki in a tight embrace. "I heard somebody giving you a hard time. Lead me to them. I'll fuck them up."

"Easy, Kung-Fu Girl." Nicki hugged the woman, whose name was Suki, for a while, but pushed away when she tried to kiss her on the lips.

"Oh, come on. You some prude now?" She turned to me. "You don't mind do you, white boy? We'll let you watch." Everybody laughed at that, even me, though I was not sure I was getting the joke.

"We stopped by to hang out here for a few. Some place where folks don't like to look for you no how." Nicki seemed to be in charge of this group in some way. "We also need to change clothes. My boy is meeting with Anna Dare herself tonight. He's hot shit. Max leave any stuff around here he could use?" I was in full suspicion mode now. Langston brought me a shirt, some underwear, and a pair of jeans from a closet, and I followed Nicki upstairs to a room that was empty except for a futon and a TV mounted on the wall. I announced that I hadn't slept great and needed to take a nap.

"That's a good idea. You need to be on your game tonight." She kissed me. "Don't worry about these crazies. They good folks on our side." She kissed me again and closed the door. I Looked around for a while not knowing what I was looking for, maybe cameras. After waiting five long minutes, I sat down on the linoleum floor with my back leaning against the door and texted Jill Devereaux.

How do you know she isn't who she says she is?
Took you long enough. I was worried.
How do you know?
I'm a reporter, dumbo. I hear shit.
Who is she?
Our Nicki is some kind of Black Ops person for some scary agency
that doesn't exist on paper.
You're crazy.
Maybe. But I've been doing some checking, and Nicole Rice didn't
exist in her current form a year ago.
She saved my ass twice in the last week. People jumped us last night
after we left your place.
Really? Wonder if they were after you or her?
Who is your source for this?
Can't say, lover. But let's just say that Anna's people know some-
thing. Nicki's cleaned her last toilet there.
I can't believe this. She could take the manuscript from me any time
she wanted. She has a gun.
That's a puzzlement for me, as well. Not sure about her angle there.
She must need you for something.

Great.

*You're in a bad place. My advice would be to give up that notebook
     to Anna and head back to Alabama or Mississippi and lay low.*
          I will see that you get paid for it.
I think Nicki's coming with me.
Tell her you want to go alone.
Not sure how.
Be resourceful.
I need to go.

I really didn't need to go, but there was no more point texting with Jill,
and I quickly deleted the thread before undressing and lying down on
the futon as if truly napping. Jill was right, I thought, about being in
a bad place. Even if I could figure a way to get through the bars on the
window and escape, I would be in the middle of the worst part of Saint
Louis alone on foot. The notebook on the floor beside me seemed like
a curse left by my parents. I would have been fine to do nothing with
my life until I found it. I had gotten used to the idea of being a nobody
who just waits to die, but now I had been given a glimpse of something
so good it was unbelievable. My mistake was believing in it. I got up
and went out into the hallway where I could barely hear Nicki's voice
from below. Going to the top of the steps, I could almost hear Suki
reply in a passionate voice.

"Lang and Max and me are the same on this. You are our girl, and
we do what we do like always. But if you fuck this up we get the collat-
eral shit jammed hard up our asses." Nicki tried to speak with no success
as Suki raised her voice. "I'm willing to die for a reason, but not a dumb
one because you need a pysch evaluation or some shit."

"There is a reason." This was another voice from Nicki I had not
heard, a voice of authority. "If you don't trust me on this, you should

close up shop today. Say I lost it, say whatever you need to protect your-selves." Suki made a sound of disgust.

"Fuck you. Just don't fuck us." From the way she said it, I could tell that the conversation was over, and I hurried back to the room. I was alone for another half hour trying to make sense of what I had heard. When Nicki finally came up, opening the door slowly as if to avoid wak-ing me, I wondered if she was ready to tell me who she was.

"This is all they got for me, but beggars can't be choosers." She was wearing a white lace dress with a faded jean jacket. When she hugged me, I could feel the lump of the gun in the pocket. I did not kiss her or caress her, and she noticed.

"How do you know these guys? Who are they?" She hesitated before answering.

"Just some folks I know from back in the day." She cupped my chin. "They real cool. Long as we're cool." I took it as a threat, even though she was smiling as she said it. To make matters worse, she snaked onto my lap making me feel both powerful and weak at the same time as if she had pulled out the gun and dropped to her knees.

"Should we get out of here?" I wanted to break the spell she had over me that even with all I knew made me feel lucky to hold her. I was still hoping that Jill Devereaux was wrong. I was in love.

"Where you want to go? It has to be some place real public where nobody will try nothing."

"How about the Zoo?" She laughed and checked a text that had just buzzed on her phone.

"Yeah, I don't think anyone will try anything there except maybe the chimps." She slid slowly off my lap just as some loud hip-hop started playing on the lower level. As we came down the steps, Suki was going through some intense dance moves in the living room while Langston worked on his computer. Her robe, which was actually too big for her, had trouble staying with her gyrations, and her shoulders were mostly exposed. She spoke to me as we went by.

"Hey, boy. Homegirl tell you she was almost a seal?" She turned to Nicki. "By the way, how'd did a part black girl learn to swim good enough to do that? Don't cha got to be in the water once and a while?" Nicki suddenly joined her for a few seconds in a dance and they both moved the way girls did on Ecstasy.

"I guess my arms and legs are the white part."

"But your ass must float good." Nicki gave her a little finger wave good-bye as she danced to the door. Suki used both hands to finger us as she kept dancing. Outside, Max was just pulling up in her Challenger. He did not smile at either of us, but accepted Nicki's fist bump.

"You take care of my baby?" She pointed at her car that seemed freshly waxed.

"At least it's not all shot to shit like my car." He handed her the keys after she gave him the keys to the Hyundai.

"Be careful in there. Suki's getting herself all worked up." The music was pretty loud where we were standing.

"Everyone getting worked up. Bad idea." He looked at me saying "Nice shirt" before he walked away.

Chapter 24

YATES

"I never understood the whole Jill Devereaux connection. Who is she? I mean if you're going to change your name, why go with that?' Yates thought that he was being funny with that remark, and Ryan found himself laughing as required. Milla cracked only the briefest of smiles. "You checked her out, this Jill, didn't you?"

"Yes. I had some people in Saint Louis look into her in the usual ways." Ryan was trying to imply that he was above such an investigation himself. "She was not affiliated with any sort of organization that might be a concern. She is just this lucky person that Anna Dare chose to make famous." Yates laughed in a not fake way.

"Amazing how that works, isn't it?" No one attempted to answer Yates' rhetorical question though he waited a few seconds before proceeding. "Some little cipher, like this Ben idiot, gets to feel significant just on the whim of Anna Dare. That's the whole point of this story, and I'm afraid it is becoming the point of this dumb exercise."

"Exercise." Milla said this in a way that imbued the word with a tiny droplet of venom. Yates seemed to notice, but did not seem to want to confront her. In any event, he was soon lost in thought, his eyes almost going dead in the process. Ryan said nothing so as not to interrupt his process that went on for several minutes. When he spoke, however, he made no great pronouncement.

"Read some more of this to me."

Chapter 25

BEN FORD

"I know how to get to the park from here." Nicki said this because I was searching on my phone as we headed back up Goodfellow. "Are you taking Kingshighway?"

"Can." She was almost annoyed, but I wanted to see how much.

"I want to stop at a Post Office near Lindell." She raised her eyebrows. "I want to put this notebook in the mail. I think we'd be crazy to take it to this meeting tonight."

"Good thinking." That was all she said as she turned on Delmar and we caught the edge of the Loop. The people on the street there were white, black, and Asian, with several hijabs and even a turban in the mix. The only demographic that was constant was they were all young and looked hungry for life. We didn't talk much on the trip, and I couldn't tell if she was hurt that I didn't trust her to leave the notebook with her friends. She seemed indifferent. She waited in the car as I went into the Post Office. I pulled a number from the dispenser and called my grandparents in Florida.

"Hello?" My grandmother did not like phone calls from people she did not recognize, and my number was definitely not one that would show up on her phone. I was glad I had loaded their number into mine.

"Grandma. It's Ben." I knew if I hesitated saying my name she would hang up thinking I was a dreaded telephone solicitor.

"Ben!" Her excitement waned quickly. "Where are you? Is everything all right? Did Erin get in touch with you about selling that house?"

"Everything is fine, Grandma." I told her about the quick sale, and she seemed very impressed with her go-getter granddaughter who was looking out for her dumb cousin. She asked if I wanted to talk to my grandfather about where to invest the money before "it all just slips away." I would have to call later as he was out just then. I said I needed to ask for a favor.

"Favor?"

"I want to mail you a package to hold for me. Would that be OK?" There was a long silence.

"I guess that would be all right." She sounded confused.

"Do me another favor and don't open it or anything until I come down there."

"You're coming for a visit?" She had mixed feelings. She liked the idea of having her grandson visit, but she was not sure about my motives.

"In a few days, yes. I will fly down and pick up the package. And take you and grandpa out to dinner somewhere nice. He and I can talk investment strategies then."

"It's not drugs, is it?"

"No, Grandma. It's nothing like that." I suppose every grandma thinks guys like me go to drugs unless we are married and have a regular job. It's mostly true, I guess.

"It's something very special that Uncle Al left me that I want you to hold onto for me. I am just afraid I will lose it with all of these emotional things I am dealing with." She went to full grandma mode and agreed. I triple checked her address before signing off just as they called my number.

"Would you like to insure this?" The postal employee had put the note-book in a little shipping box and waited patiently while I wrote my grand-parent's address and my uncle's return address on the outside. I considered insuring it for a ridiculous sum, but thought that might seem stupid since he had already seen that the content of the box was nothing special. I walked out with the tracking number in my pocket half expecting that Nicki had left, but she was right in the parking lot looking at her phone.

"Let's go see the lions, player."

Even though school was still in session, Forest Park, where the Zoo is located, was very crowded with cars filled with tourists and buses stuffed with students all keen to enjoy a beautiful spring day. For St. Louis kids the Zoo had always been a great cheap date even when I was growing up since for some reason admission is free. I saw a teen couple who were probably skipping school walking in front of us as we passed the birdhouse to get to the main entrance. They held hands tentatively, with their other hands gripping phones for moral support. I took Nicki's hand in imitation of them, a joke she did not acknowledge.

"Damn! I forgot about that." She said this as we stood in front of a sign that said that no firearms were allowed in the park even for people with carry permits. We stood there for a moment considering our op-tions. "I could put it back in the car, but there's people who watch for that to pop your trunk and steal it before you get to the polar bears."

"Art Museum?" I pointed up the hill.

"Yeah, I could use some culture. I don't think they sell hot dogs though."

Even though it is a short walk, we went back to the car to drive up Art Hill. They did not have hot dogs in the fancy restaurant there, but there was a good burger, even though it had something called tipsy cheddar cheese, which did not seem like a real thing. We took our time eating with Nicki mostly giving me pointers for meeting Anna Dare.

"You have never met anyone like her. She has a way of seeing things about you, things you can't see."

"So I guess I had better tell the truth." She had ordered a grilled cheese, but was barely touching it.

"It ain't like that. She doesn't care if you lie to her about some this or that." Nicki had taken off her jean jacket to reveal her bare arms in the sleeveless dress. The waiter seemed half in love with her before we ordered, and two old ladies next to us were actually staring at her the whole time as if they might have sighted a celebrity.

"She doesn't care if you lie to her?" Nicki seemed about to let her guard down. I was wondering what lie she had told Anna Dare. She shook her head.

"She only cares about the Truth that is in you." She stopped herself before going on. "Shit, I do sound crazy as some of these folks around here." She pushed her plate away. "Listen, Ben. You should just get rid of this thing your parents wrote as soon as you can and forget all this stuff that has happened."

"About you too?" She did not really protest that thought.

"This has been a pretty fast pace, you got to admit. Maybe…" we were interrupted by one of the old women suddenly appearing at our table.

"I apologize if we have been rude in staring at you, but we just couldn't get over you sitting here with that Delacroix print right behind you." I turned to look at it. The walls of the café, of course, were covered with art, but this painting of a young woman did have a striking resemblance to Nicki. They told us it was called "Orphan Girl at the Cemetery." We had a polite conversation about other strange things that happened to the old woman during her life. After she left, Nicki was in no mood to talk.

We did walk briefly through the museum, which reminded me of a junior high field trip which was the last time I had been there. We wound up in a room with very modern stuff that just made me think of chaos. All the colors brought to mind blood and gore, and the lines seemed inexact as if nothing could ever be depicted as it was because nothing truly existed. The other sections of the museum with medieval Christian art or even the Renaissance portraits seemed too old to reference anything. The encounter with the old woman seemed to have upset Nicki, and I would have found a way to ask her if she had been an orphan, but I was thinking too much about myself. After a while, I announced that I needed to find the men's room, and she announced that she would wait outside having had her fill of culture. In the bathroom I texted Jill to tell her that we were still together, and I had no plan. An old guy came in while I was waiting for an answer and shook his head at the millennial that has to text in the can. When Jill texted back, she said my situation would be "handled."

Nicki was beneath the statue of Saint Louis talking on the phone when I exited the museum. The view was pretty cool from there, the lagoon at the bottom with its fountains looking as it did during the big World's Fair in another century. My parents took me sledding down the great slope when I was maybe eight or so. We all went down together in a frenzy of laughter and fear and togetherness. My father said, "Marie hold on tight," as we started down though that was not my mother's name. Remembering it years later, I looked that up to find out it was from some poem, but I have forgotten it and have no access to the internet.

"I wonder if Anna got hung up in California." Nicki said that as I came close. She had ended her call, but before I could say anything, my phone rang. I was hoping it wasn't Jill doing something dumb. A man quickly identified himself as Steven Yates and asked to whom he was speaking.

"This is Ben Ford." I tried to sound like someone to be taken seriously, but it was a stretch for me.

"Good. Anna looks forward to meeting with you this evening."

"What time?"

"Oh, why, now would be an excellent time if you are free." I made some sound to indicate that I was free. "There is just one thing. We would prefer that you came by yourself. We have implemented some new security measures just now and that would be for the best. Are you good with that?" I said I was and hung up.

"I can go now, but he wants me to come alone."

"Does he?" Nicki was looking out past the lagoon to the taller buildings visible just outside the park. I didn't say anything. She turned and handed me the keys without really looking at me. I thought I should say something.

"We can just go back to Saint Charles, and I can get my car." This was a weak statement, but I was very confused about her just then. Ever since the post office, her attitude toward me had changed or at least that was what I thought.

"Nah, I'll just let you off there at Anna's, and you can text me when you get done." She turned around and walked toward the car. She pointed up at the statue of Saint Louis that loomed above us, about to swing his drawn sword. "I always think he's ready to go on a killing spree like Michael Myers or some psycho. Welcome to the city, you sinners!" She didn't laugh and neither did I.

Chapter 26

BEN FORD

She let me drive. The Challenger had too much power and seemed to physically reject the low speeds I was going as we snaked through the park to get to Kingshighway. The big street became poorer as we headed north away from the sprawling Barnes Hospital complex, the fancy apartments, the gated streets. In only a few minutes driving time more buildings were empty and abandoned. We passed a White Castle with a long crack in its window covered with tape and a boarded up church of some denomination I had never heard of. I gigged the car just a little as we pulled onto Highway 70 with immediate joy at the jolt of power, but also an anxiety that it might be too much to control which made me slow down.

"You getting nervous?" Nicki said this just as the rain began popping on the windshield. We had been silent on the drive with both of us sensing that something was wrong. The seeds of doubt were growing as if the rain nurtured them as it began to fall heavily enough for me to turn on the wipers once I located them.

"I guess I am a little nervous." She did not reply and we were mostly quiet except for her giving me directions. As I drove, I had been thinking that I would shortly out the answers to two big questions in my life all before the night was over. Anna Dare, who I imagined to be a fraud, would either make me stupid rich or not. Either way, I would ask Nicki to go with me the next morning to Florida racing the post office delivery to my grandparents. If she agreed, I was willing to think that Jill Devereaux was crazy with all this talk about Black Ops (which did seem crazy). I felt a strange peace in being about to know those things, the resolution of a man about to hear the foreman of the jury read his verdict, so he could get on with the finality of prison or the joy of freedom.

When we arrived in Ferguson, the traffic on Florissant Road was slowed to a crawl with the heavy rain making the last part of the journey to Anna's house seem to take forever. Nicki told me to turn on a street called Calverton Road that had some large houses that appeared mostly well cared for from what I could tell. Even if she wouldn't have told me which one was Anna Dare's house, I would have figured it out. There was a new looking chain link fence around the perimeter of one that extended to the edge of the front sidewalk. A large section on the side was stuffed with rolled up pieces of paper in the links of the fence. I had read that people put notes in there telling their stories of woe, requesting money. Supposedly they were all retrieved and brought to Anna every night and placed in a pile from which she selected the ones that she felt worthy by her powers of intuition. I assumed that today's hopes were slowly dissolving in the rain.

The house was an old 1940s style sprawling ranch that was set way back from the street. It must have been a big deal back in the day, but probably not a hot property for many, many years. Only a black sawhorse blocked the entrance to the driveway though halfway up an SUV was parked sideways as a real deterrent. When I pulled in right up to the sawhorse, two men in blue windbreakers exited the SUV and came toward us. Nicki and I got out of the car and waited for them in what had slowed to a gentle sprinkle.

"I'm Ben Ford. I think I have an appointment." They nodded. One asked for my ID, which he examined with a flashlight.

"Bob not working tonight?" Nicki said this to the one not checking my license who acted amused that she knew Bob.

"There have been some changes. Bob's been reassigned." They both seemed amused now. The one handed my license back and turned to Nicki.

"I'm sorry. Mr. Ford is the only one on the list."

"So I heard." She gave me a brief hug. "Text me when you're done, and I'll be here in a flash. Now go with God." As she got back in her car, I could feel that everything had changed though I was still hoping it hadn't. She laughed a little when she said, "Go with God," and I was hoping that was all she found funny as she drove away leaving me alone.

Chapter 27

BEN FORD

They security boys ran a wand over me and asked that I remove my keys and phone for examination. After a brief call on a walkie-talkie, one of them led me up to the big oak front door that was quickly opened by an older, friendlier man who identified himself as Bob. The three of us stood there talking about the rain the way men do when they are strangers, though the other security guy, who did not offer his name, mostly just nodded. In the small front room there was only one chair on which a copy of *The Way* lay open waiting for Bob to return to it. When I heard footsteps coming around the corner, I expected to see Anna Dare, but a somewhat distinguished gray-haired man appeared instead.

"Good evening, Mr. Ford!" He wore black jeans and a sport coat with leather patches on the elbows, and he extended his hand as he approached. "I'm Steven Yates. I apologize for all this security, but such is the world nowadays." He was friendly and all, but had sort of an intimidating presence the way a big time college professor can be as he waits to be disappointed by how much you don't know about whatever subject he taught.

"No problem." I lapsed right into my undergraduate way of talking, and he seemed to have his suspicions confirmed enough to smile sympathetically. He indicated that I should follow him into the bowels of the house as the two security men left us alone. The place was old, but it looked as if everything, even the wood floors had been recently redone. Passing the very modern kitchen, we saw a woman in yoga pants and a tank top peeling a banana. I hesitated, thinking it was Anna, since she resembled the pictures I had seen on the web with a great mass of hair for a woman over 50 tied on top of her head. Yates was quick to correct my misunderstanding.

"That is Justine, Anna's amanuensis, fitness trainer, and the person who keeps this place from descending into chaos on a daily basis." Justine said nothing, only giving me a brief sort of bow with her hands in front of her still holding the banana. Yates tugged at my arm gently, but firmly, leading me quickly away. We entered a sunken family room that was also very large for an old house, and I wondered whether some walls had been knocked out to accommodate the square footage. The first thing I noticed was a blood red area rug with white butterflies woven throughout. There were two large chocolate brown leather couches at opposite ends of the room and several strange looking chairs that seemed more like works of art than something you could sit on. The picture of King Kong grabbing on to the Arch was mounted above the fireplace, so I guess someone had retrieved it from Violet's Café that week. Above each of the leather couches was a very large painting, one featured a small boat being tossed about in a violent storm, while the other was maybe the same boat sailing calmly on a sea of glass in bright sunlight. I thought they were about order and chaos, but that was the last thought I had before Anna Dare entered the room, and all focus shifted to her.

"Ben! It must be you!" She was also dressed for yoga, but her black t-shirt had those four words, "learning, accomplishment, kindness, plea-sure" printed in a slightly lighter shade of black making them almost invisible until she was very close. I held out my hand, but she pushed it aside and hugged me with such force that I almost lost my balance. Anna smelled of flowers as if she had just walked through a garden.

"Mr. Ford appears to be associated with Ms. Nicki Rice since he arrived with her this evening." Yates said that as soon as she broke off the long embrace. I guess he had been watching or one of the security guys had told him.

"Good for him associating with such a beauty." Anna sat on the couch nearest us patting it with her hand to indicate that I should sit next to her. "Now please leave me alone with this young man as we have some things to work out between us." When Yates seemed about to protest, she waved her hand at him. "Don't worry. He seems unlikely to strangle me just yet. Are you?" I shook my head, and the man made a little bow and left.

Anna Dare is the most famous person I have ever actually met, much less sat next to alone. Most not famous people, who ever encoun-ter someone like her, want to document the moment with a selfie to prove later that they had actually occupied the same small shred of the universe with that person at the same time. Usually the celebrity, bored but resigned, allows only a few seconds in his presence before moving on. I was sitting next to the most famous woman, maybe person, in the world who showed no hurry to be anywhere else. Sitting in a sideways lotus position, she allowed her knee to touch my hip as if I had known her all my life.

"So your Uncle Al told me you were an atheist. Is that so?" With her hair pulled back and no make-up, she looked like any attractive woman in her fifties, but not really anything special. Just before I answered her question I looked into her eyes for the first time, and saw, or sort of felt, what everyone writes about who has met her. Although her eyes are an interesting blue-green color, they are not so much beautiful as piercing as if they see directly into your mind at the same time that they invite you into a world that you desperately want to exist. She did have some African-American features, and she somewhat reminded me of that older woman who was the first black Miss America a long time ago, a person accustomed to being looked at. As I reread this, it might sound as if I felt some sexual tension in the situation with a famous woman barefoot within inches of me, but nothing like that crossed my mind.

"You talked about me with my uncle?" I tried to look away from her eyes, but it was not easy.

"We did, especially about your lack of belief. I told him not to worry about you just yet." I noticed that she offered me no condolences for his death as she tapped me lightly on the shoulder. "There are no atheists, you know."

"I think I know pretty many." I said this without really thinking in a way to combat the effect she was having on me. If we were to negotiate, I had to seem strong, I thought. She took my hand in hers as a favorite aunt might.

"God is whatever you value, and everyone who chooses to live values something. The people who desire only wealth or fame or some sort of power know full well the gods they serve, those that speak to them constantly." I had a feeling that she was inviting me to question her, so I did.

"The difference, I think, is that no one claims that those gods actually exist or sets up a religion devoted to them." I kept trying to look at the gold hoop on her right ear to avoid those eyes.

"You think so?" She touched her ear as if she knew I was staring at it. "I think that all those lucky charms, amulets, lit candles, prayers, and whatever are just attempts to control God for some personal advantage." She tapped my nose. "Those who have read my book know that they always have a connection to God in the way they live their lives. They have been touched by the miracle of the words. The words that express what they already feel in their hearts."

"I guess. But it would be too bad if those words were found out to be plagiarized." I wanted to put that out there to see what happened. She leaned back a little out of my space and smiled.

"Technically, plagiarism could not be proven in this case. Your uncle knew that. This document you say you have was never registered in any sort of legal way." She let that sink it. "Of course, many, many people would love to find any reason to discredit my message. Al was very sensitive to that."

"So why didn't he just give it to you?" She took my hand again. I wanted to pull away, but it seemed to be such a tender gesture that I didn't stop her.

"He was about to, but he wanted to show it to you first." That hit me pretty hard so I tried to move back into negotiating to avoid thinking about my dead uncle.

"I think that my parents deserve some kind of credit for everything that is happening with this book." I wondered whether she noticed that I did not say "your" book. She squeezed my hand tightly.

"I could easily make you a rich man by paying you for the notebook, but I don't feel the need to do it," she pulled my hand to her mouth and kissed one of my knuckles, "at least not just yet." I did pull my hand away then.

"It seems to me that there are some people who have no problems making me a rich man if I would sell it to them." I stood up as if I was ready to leave. With me out of the way Anna stretched out the length of the couch regarding me.

"I can't tell if you remind me more of your mother or your father or just a wonderful amalgam of both." Her eyes were back on mine, and we were silent for a minute. "You poor boy. It must have been dreadful for you to lose all that love at once, to feel the world go from full to empty in such a flash."

Those words froze the blood in my veins. I had thought some version of them a million times, but never said them aloud for fear the raw truth would be unbearable. In just that moment I hated, feared, and loved Anna Dare all at the same time. Her eyes now reflected my pain and maybe absorbed some from me. It is impossible for me to adequately describe the emotions that flooded my brain, and I felt almost like my ten-year-old self hearing the news of their death.

"I don't really remember. I was just a kid." That was the lie that I told people, but she just smiled at it as if I was still a kid. I wanted to change the subject. "You knew my parents?" She fished two fun-sized Milky Ways from a bowl on the end table tossing me one before unwrapping the other.

"I knew them well before you were conceived when the three of us were all so impossibly young." She popped the candy into her mouth and spent a while consuming it before going on. "I knew your mom from Wash U and your dad used to hang out with a guy I dated who was also into motorcycles." She moved her feet back slightly to allow me to sit down and eat my Milky Way.

"Are we talking in the 90s?"

"In the early 90s, yes, with all those REM and Nirvana songs on the radio as the Berlin wall was coming down. It was such a great time to be young and full of life." She picked up two more Milky Ways bopping me in the head with one of them. "It was on a Labor Day weekend, I remember, just as the summer was giving up the ghost that we all went to my uncle's house in the Ozarks." She must have noticed that I was just nodding as she went on.

"There was a bonfire and some substances to fuel the fires inside us.

Valerie had recently had a break with the Catholic Church for various reasons, and I think that started us on a deep religious discussion."

"Ah." I was picturing my parents, younger than I was by many years, having one of those stoned college chats that never happen later in life. I loved thinking about them that way and having my mother called "Valerie" by a famous person. It might seem stupid, but I did.

"Your mother got us going by arguing, in that way she had, that any concept of God had to be unchanging throughout history. I came up with the idea that it must be an idea that could be embraced by even the lowest of the low, the greatest sinners in the world." She hesitated a second while she studied her Milky Way as if looking at it was part of the ritual of eating it. "Then Jack, your father, who was sort of teasing us about reading Spinoza and Wittgenstein, said that whatever the concept was, it had to be graspable by even the simplest of minds, even those who could not read anything." She locked her eyes on me then, and I did not turn away.

"The next part you probably won't believe, but it happened. We were staring at the fire, and a voice uttered the four words, 'kindness, accomplishment, learning, pleasure" in a matter-of-fact sort of way. Valerie and I both thought the other had said them, yet neither of us had spoken. We were scared a little that someone had snuck up through the woods. After a brief search, we decided we had received a revelation. We were moved, not in the ecstatic way you might expect after hearing the voice of God, but inspired to do something about it. We stayed up all night and wrote the first three chapters of *The Way*."

"You all wrote it?" This, of course, made the whole plagiarism idea even more foolish. To be honest, at that moment, if I would have had the notebook with me, I would have given it to Anna Dare; I was drawn to her. Some of this was the way she spoke of my parents, a way no one ever spoke of them, but much of it was just Anna's presence in the room, the feeling that she cared about me, her eyes, her naked feet projecting both intimacy and saintliness.

"Yes. We continued to work on it over the next several weeks as if guided by a divine power." Her eyes were closed now giving herself over to the memory.

"And you never did anything with it? For all those years?"

"We tried some, but to no avail. We were so young, and we didn't know anyone who could help us." She opened her eyes. "And no one wanted to touch a story inspired by some God that didn't fit any mold of previous gods written by a bunch of college kids."

"So you forgot about it, or my parents forgot about it?" I was thinking about my mother telling me all those Psalms every night. She had not forgotten.

"It was always with me." She thought a second. "I, unfortunately, lost track of your parents after I moved to Europe shortly after that summer to start living another life. It was so easy to lose people before the internet demolished all the distance in the world."

"So, I guess I should just give it to you. My parents, I somehow think, would have wanted me to do that." I was speaking like a child and felt like one. She sat up.

"I will accept it from you, but I want more." She spread her arms wide. "I am about to change the whole world forever, and I want you to be a part of that. Nothing will be what it was, all because of this book that your parents and I wrote together." She took my hand again. "I want their DNA beside me, and it resides in you, my dear."

I think that sounds creepier on the page than it was in real life. She seemed to want to adopt me more than anything else. I was so moved by the intensity of Anna Dare, by her knowing my parents, caring about them, that I don't remember clearly what we talked about after that. I only remember the sound of her voice. It brought back a memory of my mother whispering into my neck as I sat on her lap, a sound of pure love. It was all too much. At some point, I was afraid that I might start sobbing like an idiot.

"I'm sorry. I have to go." I stood up and moved to the center of the big room before turning back to her. "It will take me a few days to get the notebook." She held up her hand.

"No great hurry after all these years. You read it first very carefully. Then you decide if you want to be a part of all this." She (I swear it) bowed her head toward me, a bow that made two strands of her hair fall around her face. "It is your choice."

"I don't…" I was still looking at the top of her head, and no words came to me. She came forward and took me in her arms.

"Dear boy. I would love to pay you to give it to me because you are their son. Maybe I will, but I want it to mean more to you than that." She touched my cheek ever so gently. "You need to want something that can't be bought and that no one can give you." Those were the last words she said to me that day before she released me and turned toward the hallway.

"Bob!" In a forceful tone, she called the security guy who appeared very quickly to escort me out of the house. Anna Dare said nothing else to me that night, not even good-bye. Bob took my arm as if he sensed that I needed steadying after the encounter. He was right.

Chapter 28

YATES

"That settles it. You are going to Saint Louis tomorrow, young man, if we can't get you on a red-eye tonight." Yates turned to Milla. "Book him whatever is available." She dutifully picked up her phone.

"Maybe we should hear everything before we make firm plans." Ryan was not certain, given the rest of the story that he wanted to go.

"It doesn't matter what happens, pardner. I need you on the ground getting this clusterfuck under control. You got that?" Ryan wondered whether he should keep disagreeing to get fired, but he had too much riding on this. If he did fix it, he would be golden in the man's eyes.

"Yes, sir."

"You have a flight tomorrow out of SFO at 6:30 AM." Milla looked only at her phone as she said this.

"Let's wrap this insanity up, Dear Reader." There was no mirth at all in his words, and Ryan regretted not just giving him a summary as he picked up the document.

Chapter 29

BEN FORD

I was outside in a renewed drizzle trying to get my bearings when Steven Yates came from around the corner carrying an umbrella. From the way he approached me I could tell that he wanted to talk, and I assumed he wanted to know how my meeting had gone. I had taken out my phone to text Nicki once I remembered that I had no car, but I stopped to greet him. He came close enough that I was covered by his umbrella, so close I could smell the tic-tac he had recently popped that was supposed to cover the smell of cigar smoke. It didn't.

"I trust that you had a successful visit with Anna. Many people would kill to get ten minutes; you had a good half hour."

"It was something." I was still pretty confused from my encounter, and something about his use of the word "kill" bothered me. I could tell he was aware of it.

"Let's have a seat in the car for a second if you don't mind. I feel awkward holding off the elements in this way." There was a black BMW sedan parked at the end of the driveway with doors that shut with a click of perfect engineering when we got in it. I had some curiosity about what he wanted.

"Your car?" It smelled new, and I was wondering what sort of salary Anna paid him.

"I drive it some, but technically it belongs to her," he wagged his head toward the house, "as does everything here." He cleared his throat. "I am sorry about your uncle. I met him once, and he seemed like a good man."

"He was." Something made me want to knock him off his high horse. "I just hope his involvement with Anna Dare didn't get him killed." He sighed.

"I don't know. There are many people who want to hurt Anna for obvious reasons, religious fanatics of every stripe, and even some very mainstream people who want to silence her message." He was looking at the dashboard as he spoke. "People, the wrong people, may have found out that your uncle had something, and they were determined to get it, even if it was just for some financial gain."

"Or they may have been Anna's people who wanted to silence his message." I was just starting to feel my own guilt in his death from what Anna had just told me. If he hadn't waited for me to see the notebook before he gave it away, he might still be alive. Of course, I was still hoping that his death had been natural causes, but I wanted to see if Yates would react. He did not.

"There are many bad actors in the world and quite a few of them have relocated to the Saint Louis area since Anna's revelation. I am sad to say you could be right." He looked straight at me now as the rain started up strong after a blast of lightning. "How long have you known Nicki Rice, our putative cleaning lady?"

"Just this week." It took me a second to remember what "putative" meant, and I sort of knew where this was heading.

"She, above all, is a very dangerous person."

"So I've heard." I was trying to act tough, but wasn't feeling it. He leaned closer and lowered his voice as if someone might be outside the car in the pouring rain listening to us.

"She is a member of a very secret organization located deep in the bowels of the government. It is a group that reports to no one that you have ever heard of, a group that is authorized to do any terrible thing it wants without consequence." He actually looked a little scared, but it might have been an act.

"How do you know this?" I was wondering if Jill Devereaux was the source of all these rumors for some reason I couldn't comprehend.

"I know because I requested her to be here." He ran his fingers through his long, gray hair. "I have some friends who know all the workings of this world, who put me in touch with someone who could assign a team to protect Anna against any threats."

"Any?"

"Look, you don't know how many people hate Anna and have pledged to do her harm. She won't agree to the large security team that we need so some friends with connections located a government organization that specializes in deploying a very small team capable of big things."

"So Nicki does work for the government?"

"Yes, but she seems to have gone rogue, and her superiors feel that she is no longer under their control." He looked toward the house. "Something about Anna may have triggered her in some way, though from what I have recently learned she was already a very dangerous person."

"Dangerous to who?"

"All of us." He slumped his shoulders. "This is my fault. I trusted some people that this Nicki would just be some added security that Anna would not need to know about." He hesitated. "Now I don't know what sort of monster I may have summoned, but I know some things she has done in the past."

"Like what?" I shouldn't have asked, but I did. He took a deep breath.

"Two years ago, she went undercover as a high-end escort just to get close to the leader of the most dangerous narco-terrorist cartel in South America. After some months, she managed to ingratiate herself with his number one man and was eventually flown to a secret compound in the rainforest where the kingpin stayed. After a night of unthinkable debauchery, she calmly slaughtered his bodyguards, and sent out some sort of signal to the authorities who found the criminal hog-tied and blindfolded in his pool house." He put a hand on my shoulder. "You don't know who, or what, you have been dealing with."

"There is no way this is true. There is no group like that in America." He gave me his smug professor look, the one for students that don't quite get it.

"Call her and ask her." He opened his car door, sticking out his arm to open the umbrella. "Just be careful. She just might say or do anything." He left me alone in the Beemer. I thought about faking a call, but decided to go ahead and do it. She answered on the first ring.

"You all done with the prophet?" Her voice was cheerful enough with just a touch of the concern from earlier.

"Nicki." I took a deep breath. "Who are you?"

"Jesus, what are you talking about?"

"Are you working for the government for some super-secret CIA, FBI organization?" She did not laugh as I was hoping.

"Who told you that?" Her voice was sad, but I was not sure what she was sad about.

"Two different people." I could feel myself losing it. Has this whole thing been just bullshit to get close to me, to make me do whatever you want?"

"What would I want you to do?"

"Who knows? I don't know anything." Anna Dare had really loosened my usually tight grip on my emotions, which were getting the best of me. I raved at her for a while. When I asked her if she had been keeping things from me she did laugh in a scary way.

"Nobody ever tells you everything, player." She let that grim news sink in. "Now, let me come by and get you. You still at Anna's? We'll go get something to eat, and I'll tell you more than you ever need to know about shit. Just wait there." Something about her last statement seemed like an order, and I was not in the mood for orders just then. I hung up and turned the sound on my phone off. After a few vibrations, Yates returned, and seeing I was not holding my phone, got back in.

"What did she say?'

"None of your fucking business." I was pretty crazy just then, and I immediately regretted the harshness of my words though he seemed to take no offense. "Sorry. I'm still trying to process all of this."

"It's a lot, I suppose, for all of us." He pulled out a key fob with the BMW logo on it. "My friend, you need to get out of town for a few days, and not see this Nicki, or whatever her name is, until I do some more checking and have her called off." He handed me the fob.

"I can take your car?"

"It is Anna's, as I said, and she gives away things much more expensive than this every day." He again patted me on the shoulder. "Take all the time you need. Just drop it off when you figure out what you want to do. Knowing Anna, I suspect she will just give it to you." He got out and let me into the driver's seat, still in a daze. He waved to the security guys to let me out tapping the roof of the BMW as I went by. I am surprised that I made it through Ferguson back to Highway 70 without having an accident.

Most of my thoughts were terrible. It was possible that Anna Dare had bewitched me, the way that charismatic cult leaders do. She might never have known my parents at all and come into possession of a copy of the manuscript a hundred different ways. Of course the Nicki thing was killing me, not so much that she was a secret agent (I really didn't believe that), but more that all my doubts about someone like her having any real interest in me seemed true. Even driving that BMW, I felt that I was worse off than a week ago when I had just been moving furniture with every day like the one before it and no thoughts of the future. Some old guy in a bar once told me that the ability to imagine a better life was the greatest cause of depression. As I drove west away from Ferguson and got to Highway 70, I was thinking just how right that was.

Highway 70, as I mentioned, crosses over the Missouri River and continues to Kansas City and all the way to Utah. I took it for a while until I got hungry and exited when a sign advertised one of the local landmark Steak n' Shake restaurants that were a staple of my youth. I decided to eat one last St. Louis meal before leaving town.

Chapter 30

BEN FORD

I sat on a stool at the counter where people dined alone and ordered a burger and one of the great milkshakes that reminded me of the hunger of youth that feared no calories. Noticing the Wal-Mart that loomed in the distance, I had planned to go there and buy various things for a short trip with some tiny satisfaction in not caring how much I spent; even with all the troubling things that were happening in my life, I am ashamed to admit that Yates and even Anna implying that I might still become rich kept my mood from being absolutely black. I watched the harried grill man, a guy about my age with indecipherable tattoos covering both forearms, as he responded to each order and wondered if he thought that he was a failure. As I slurped away on my shake, I thought how recently I had felt like one and how easily I could again. I decided that after Wal-Mart I was going to find a bar and get drunk.

At that time of the evening, the place was not very crowded, and the middle-aged woman who took my order had time to carry on a jokey conversation with two guys well into their 70s sitting just down from me. She was checking out customers at the register with the same cheery banter as if there was no place else she would rather be. When I had finished, I told her to keep the change from the twenty I had left on the counter. She blew me a kiss, and I saw the Dare beads slide down her wrist toward her elbow.

I was still thinking about her as I walked to my car and whether she would consider completing her shift at Steak n' Shake as an accomplishment. I was also thinking about how to get to Wal-Mart and what particular form of alcohol I might consume in the next half hour, which made me not notice the guy in the SUV next to mine who opened his door just as I was opening mine. I remember feeling relieved that I had not put a ding on a BMW that belonged to someone else while at the same time wondering why the guy had been just sitting in his car. Then lightning struck me. Someone from behind me had popped the prongs of a Taser into my back causing my muscles to freeze in a spasm of uselessness.

Within seconds that seemed like minutes, I was in the back of the SUV face down on the seat as my hands were pulled behind my back and snapped into handcuffs. I was still gasping for air as a black bag went over my head. When my tongue finally thawed out, I tried to speak though no real words came out of my mouth.

"Shut the fuck up or I'll tase your ass again." I shut the fuck up, and the car lurched and picked up speed, as we must have gone back on the highway.

We drove for what seemed like forever in my terrorized state with no one saying a word. The car radio must have been on a 70s nostalgia station with all the Eagles and Steely Dan and such playing the whole way. Being so old and dated, the songs seemed to me like dirges, which only increased my anxiety about what might happen next. Eventually, we slowed to a crawl as "Bat out of Hell" played until someone turned it off. I supposed we were there when I heard a garage door close behind us, a door that was in such desperate need of lubrication that its movement was a shriek.

I was not walking perfectly being blind and still messed up from all those volts going through me, but they got me in the house and down to a basement without knocking me off my feet. After they put me on a metal chair, I heard them clumping back up the wooden steps. There was no other sound except my heavy breathing which I was trying to get control of to prevent throwing up that milk shake. All of a sudden, I heard the sound of someone moving toward me and felt fingers on my hood. When it was pulled over my head, I was staring at a big man wearing a very creepy clown mask right in front of me.

"Here is how your life is going to work now, my friend." His accent sounded clipped like somebody from the east coast. "I am going to tell you what I want you to do, and you are going to convince me that you ready to do exactly what I say. Otherwise, we will not be close friends. You get what I'm telling you?"

"Yes." I wish I could tell you that I said something sarcastic and cutting back to him, but I didn't. You might think you would be tough in such circumstances. I might have thought so until I was in handcuffs in front of a guy with a pretty mean voice wearing a clown mask; I was not. Maybe I had not recovered from the Taser, but the only thing I could think of was sitting in Steak n' Shake less than an hour earlier listening to that waitress without comprehending just how wonderful that moment was. Clown guy could tell I was not focusing on my situation, so he smacked me hard on my temple.

"Pay attention." He was wearing some heavy leather gloves, and he put the finger of one of them against my nose. It smelled new and cheap. "So, you got any idea what's going on here."

"Right here?"

"No, stupid. I mean with this whole Anna Dare thing." I thought he was going to smack me again, and I tensed up. He must have realized that, so he moved a little away to sit and let my fear factor lower enough to hear him.

"I know who Anna Dare is." He laughed at that.

"Congratulations, Chief. You know what every swingin' dick on the planet knows." He leaned back probably wondering whether I was dumb or just scared. "Do you know how she got to be who she claims to be?"

"No." I could tell he was dying to tell me.

"So here's what we know." His voice changed as if he was going to become the good cop now to gain my trust. I was still terrified even with his new tone of voice. "Fifteen years ago or so Steven Yates wrote some stupid paper at Washington University about the impending death of the secular way of life, that he called 'The End of the Age of Reason.' Heard of it?"

"No." I actually wanted to laugh at this tough guy who seemed ready to torture me 30 seconds earlier now using the word "secular" in a sentence. I didn't.

"No one else did either or ever would have, but little Steven's big brother is one of the richest people that you also have never heard of. He runs some hedge fund or other out of New York and has more money than God." He laughed at his own brilliant joke. "Anyway, he read his kid brother's thesis and shared it with a bunch of other stupidly rich guys who he hangs out with, and they all chipped in to start something called the Messiah Project. Anybody tell you about that?"

"No, nobody told me anything." People of my generation who went to high school every day with the anticipation of some shooter with an assault rifle, have developed a knack for coping with dangerous, crazy people who might not decide to kill us later if we don't provoke them. I was doing my best to agree with everything.

"It is a secret and a damned well-kept one at that." He let me consider this or maybe he lost his train of thought. "So this Yates also knew Anna Dare from college or somewhere, and also knew that she was some borderline schizophrenic who claimed to hear voices from beyond. He figured that he could manipulate her, make her think she had written that stupid gospel or whatever they are calling it." For some reason, he decided to remove the clown mask revealing a hatchet face with dark hairs sprouting from both nostrils that was much scarier.

"She didn't write the book?" He seemed to be able to tell that I was too ready to play along even though he didn't say anything.

"We believe that most of it was written by some group of writers, probably from New York or somewhere, and Anna Dare is either going along with the scam or is so crazy that she has been made to believe she wrote it. Yates seems to be the guy controlling her for the billionaires."

"I met him today. I think you might be right about him being in charge." Mr. Agreeable.

"Hell, he even made her think that she picked the lottery numbers that those rich boys fixed for her."

"They fixed the Powerball?" He laughed in a fake sort of way.

"These men can fix anything. They run everything. A few million dollars is less than what they earn taking a shit." He was getting worked up, so I nodded in agreement to make him go on.

"So now they have this charismatic Messiah under their control who has these four commandments that fit right into their secular philosophy, a joke philosophy, but if people really believe that Anna Dare is getting the Word direct from God, they take her seriously." He threw the mask to the concrete basement floor where it fell in such a way that it still stared at me.

"Hard to believe they could keep that covered up." He really became agitated then and started pacing back and forth as he talked.

"These people control everything. They own the mainstream and social media, and those that aren't on their payroll feel their influence. Of course, the idea of a female Messiah sits so well with the mainstream media that they have hardly investigated her." He waited until he calmed down to go on. "The only things that they don't control are our mortal souls which is where Anna Dare comes in."

"I think I see what you mean." He scowled now as if he wasn't buying my bullshit.

"You don't see what I mean just yet, my friend." He moved his chair and sat down again very close to me. "These people own 90 percent of the world, and they want the rest of us to let them keep it while we are worshipping Anna Dare. I want you to help us stop these rich bastards from stealing the concept of God for their own sick purposes."

"What do you want me to do?" My mind was in overdrive. All I had was a possibly worthless notebook which was currently in the hands of the US Postal Service, and that would probably not be enough to get me out of that basement alive. I think hatchet face could see me thinking and didn't like it. He was looking for something, but I didn't know what.

"One thing we do have is a mole in her organization that lets our group know things." He was really impressed with himself, and I felt it was a good idea to nod. It occurred to me, though I was trying not to think about it, that these might have been the guys who killed my uncle. Again, I wish I had spat in the man's face, but such things are harder than they sound. "We know that Anna Dare believes that you are some big deal in this great conspiracy. Although no one knows why, it seems that she is very hot to recruit you."

"For what?"

"I was hoping you might tell me what the psycho bitch is planning next." He was really on the verge of losing his temper, but he was struggling to control himself. "I'm getting worried about you. I was hoping that you weren't already a part of this. I was praying that you weren't already a true believer."

"I'm not." I could see he didn't believe me.

"Maybe that is so, but you need to make me think that you will help us bring down Anna Dare. You need to convince me that you want to do this for the greater good of mankind because otherwise I won't be able to trust you."

"I'll do whatever you want." He shook his head.

"I want you to think about this for a minute because your attitude is not doing it for me. I need sincerity from you that doesn't seem all desperate and fake." He put a hand on my shoulder. "Because if I don't feel that sincerity, and I'm a good judge of people, those men upstairs are going to hook your testicles up to that generator over there, and we are going to find out everything you know. After that, we will make certain that you don't help this anti-Christ in any way whatsoever." The generator that he pointed to was one of the models you walk by at Lowe's without ever imagining it clamped onto your junk. Upstairs, the music had been playing for some time, and I swear it was the same 70s radio station that I had heard in the car. In the moment that I was supposed to be considering my fate, I recognized the big guitar solo at the end of "Hotel California." There was also a strange sort of bass drum sound that I had not heard before.

"Guys?" My tormentor had heard the same thud as well. When no one answered, he yelled again before starting up the steps.

What neither of us had any way of knowing was that Nicki had located my whereabouts some time ago from a device that she had placed in the heel of my shoe. Once she had the exact house, Langston Butler had intercepted a cell phone from one of the boys upstairs ordering a Domino's pizza. Suki showed up at the same Domino's, bought a hat and t-shirt and convinced the driver to let her deliver the pizza to her friends after flashing two one hundred dollar bills. One of the men opened the door to her sweet, smiling face without noticing the 9mm with a silencer that she was holding underneath the pizza box. With two bullets in his chest, he landed hard on the floor of the entryway (that was the thud). The other guy never got out of his La-Z-Boy lounger.

"What are you doing up there?" Hatchet face, seeming more annoyed than scared, advanced up the steps only to have the door open to reveal an Asian woman wearing a Domino's hat pointing a gun at him. She fired three times knocking him to the basement floor as if she had hit him with a baseball bat. She was the last thing he ever saw in this life.

"It's me! I'm OK!" I thought the woman was Suki, but I wasn't sure. I also wasn't sure that she was done with mayhem. She came quickly down the steps looking in all directions to see if there was anyone else in the dim basement.

"Glad to hear you're OK, you stupid fuck." She helped me to my feet and up the stairs, through the carnage in the living room. The pizza box I stepped over was already soaked in blood. Outside was a white SUV with Max and Langston in the front seat both looking at their phones. Suki put me in the back seat next to a stone-faced Nicki. I wanted to kiss her, but it did not seem like the right time.

Chapter 31

YATES

"Holy shit! I don't believe this." Yates got up and started pacing around the big room eventually stopping to get himself another glass of wine. Ryan stood up and stretched while Milla performed what appeared to be some advanced yoga movement by shoving her elbows deep into the couch. She effortlessly raised her legs straight out about six inches and kept them there for what seemed like a long time.

"That person could be just another crazy idiot speculating. People like that are everywhere on the web, saying anything. It means nothing by itself." Ryan did not think that was exactly the right thing to say, but it was all he could think of.

"Of course, it might mean something that there are three dead murder victims in a house somewhere in Saint Louis." He took a big swig. "Don't multiple killings even make the news anymore unless there are double digits?"

"Not always when they are 2000 miles away. I did do a search last night, and although the bodies were found, the investigation turned up nothing." Ryan wanted to calm his boss down.

"Nothing? No connection to Anna Dare or the anti-Dare people?"

"It was not mentioned in anything I read." Yates seemed more than calm as if his aces in the hole were working as he thought they should.

"Does Ford explain who these damned people are at some point?"

"There is an explanation later." Ryan's mind was so groggy that he was not absolutely sure.

"Well then. Read on Macduff."

Chapter 32

BEN FORD

The first minutes in the car are all a blur to me. I think Max got out and drove Suki's car, which we then left in the Westport Plaza parking lot for some reason (we had only been a mile away from the spot where I used to drink illegally in high school) before all going away together. Producing some sort of tool, Nicki concentrated on picking the lock on my handcuffs while Suki removed her blood spattered Domino's shirt and replaced it with a Cardinals jersey as if I wasn't sitting next to her. She was the first person I remember speaking.

"I hope they didn't have any cameras."

"There weren't any cameras. I told you I checked." Langston, who was driving, said this from the front seat without emotion.

"I hope you did. Because I just executed three citizens to keep numb nuts' heart beating, and I am not sure how that fits with whatever the fuck our mission is this week because it keeps creeping, and I hate creepy things." She seemed entitled to some deference within the group because of what had just happened.

"Where you want to go, girl?" These were the first words Nicki spoke and seemed an attempt to calm Suki down. She did not answer for a full minute.

"Let's go downtown to Lumiere. I can drink tequila and shoot crap and zone out for a few hours." She closed her eyes as if the zoning had already begun. Max started calling to book some rooms as Langston turned toward the city. Passing the Musial Bridge, I felt my handcuffs open and fall from my wrists. I thanked Nicki, but she only nodded. In the lobby of the Lumiere, I wondered whether I should think about escaping or calling for help; I thought that would be a dumb idea from what I had just witnessed, and I wanted to talk to Nicki with everything in the open.

The room she and I checked into was pretty nice with a great view of the Arch even at night, but the bright red streaks across the carpet reminded me of the scene I had just witnessed not an hour earlier. We still didn't speak to each other for a long time. I kept rubbing the welts on my wrist as Nicki paced back and forth until she took a bottle from the mini fridge and drained it in one swallow.

"Just so you know, there was no way that I could tell you who I was or what I was doing." She fished out another bottle and snapped it open with a vengeance. "But now that you are up to your eyes in this shit, and since I don't care anymore about this job, I am going to tell you everything."

"You work for the CIA or something?" I held out my hand for what was left of the small bottle of vodka. She gave it to me shaking her head at my question.

"A guy named Peterson who was in the CIA back in 2000 got a line on the 9/11 plot from a deeply imbedded source in Saudi. He alerted all the right people in plenty of time, but no one acted on the information." She sat next to me on the bed without making contact. "After the attack went down, all the right people were deathly afraid that he would leak something."

"They could have stopped 9/11/?"

"Maybe. The important thing is that, on the one hand, they thought

Peterson was a genius, and on the other, they were willing to give him whatever he wanted to keep quiet." She took the little bottle from me and dropped it on the floor when she found it empty. "What he wanted and what he got was a small group of special ops folks that was totally autonomous and invisible to any government oversight except him and the Homeland Security Director. This group would be able to act in areas of national security without having to get approval for anything they deemed necessary to erase a threat." She snapped her fingers.

"That's the group you are in?" The words "anything they deemed necessary" were scary considering I still wasn't sure of my status.

"I was recruited by Peterson right after I washed out of the Seals for having an inappropriate relationship with my CO." She clearly wasn't holding anything back now. "He trained me not just in counter intelligence, but how to become someone else, to be able to get so close to bad guys, paranoid bad guys, that they hand you the razor that slits their throats."

"Were you someone else with me?" I could have almost laughed at the insanity of my situation. It reminded me of all final breakup conversations when the woman tells you all the things that have been going on that you never noticed except none of my ex-girlfriends, I don't think, had ever casually killed anyone. She gave me a strange look.

"Good question. I've been asking myself the same thing since that day we met." She lay down on the bed staring at the ceiling.

"And?"

"And I don't know." She looked at me now. "When they assigned my little team to run surveillance on Anna to see if there was a threat against her, I thought it sounded dumb and boring, but I knew my team needed an easy assignment. Peterson had a personal interest in the situation, and that was enough for me."

"How did you get to be her maid?" I still wasn't sure that Suki wasn't going to open the door and put a bullet in my brain before going back to the casino, but I didn't especially care if I was losing Nicki.

"Peterson got me the interview through Yates. The weird thing was that Anna just decided to pick me after an hour of conversation, none of which had anything to do with cleaning."

"Did you tell her who you were?"

"Not at all. I had a cover story, and I stuck with it the whole time." She closed her eyes now. "She seemed to buy every word of the made up life I was telling her about, but she also saw through it. She could see who I was better than I could."

"Really?" She kept her eyes closed.

"I know it sounds crazy, and I even think it's crazy. The thing is, she let me hang out at the house all the time, which was great for my purposes, but she kept talking to me about her book. Although I'd read it as part of background research, she made me believe that she was in touch with something, and that I might be in touch with something too." She reached over and took my hand. "You think I'm a sucker?"

"I understand. There is something in those eyes that get to you." I squeezed her hand and wondered if we might still be together.

"Yes, they do get to you. So anyway, I was just about to quit this whole business and get my life back to something normal when all this stuff started happening."

"My uncle?" I was still hoping she wasn't going to tell me that she was involved in his death.

"That was some of it. I had heard some chatter about him having something that Anna wanted, and he had been to see her a few times though she never talked about it. I even rented that place on his block and started cleaning his house to see what he was up to."

"Did he have a heart attack or a stroke or whatever?" There was some emotion in my voice, and she answered quickly.

"Don't know for sure, but it wasn't me or any of my team that did him in." She was reading my mind. "It could have been those boys who grabbed you though they ain't telling. I put that alarm system in his house after he died, and twice it scared off people who tried to break in looking for whatever it was they thought he had." I moved closer to her.

"Is that it? Then I showed up, and you thought I might have what everyone thought they wanted?" She put both hands on my chest, which, even though it kept me at a distance, seemed more to be a caress.

"All that just happened. It had nothing to do with my assignment." Her left hand slid to my ribs. I told her what the guy holding me in the basement had said about the billionaires who were using Anna Dare to start some new religion.

"Yeah. I heard about that, and she does seem to know a bunch of rich people." Her hand moved to my hip. "And that might explain my current problem."

"Which is?" I was hoping it wasn't me.

"Just as Anna was getting ready to go to California Peterson sent me a message through our secret channel. He said to set up a termination scenario for us to execute Anna on his order when she returned. The idea was to pin it on the any of the anti-Dare groups that we had identified."

"You have orders to kill her? I thought you were supposed to be protecting her."

"Things change real fast in my world." I was wondering if it was a good time to ask her about that narco-terrorist story. I decided against it.

"Did you get the order?"

"Yes, but I stalled saying the time wasn't right, that it was too risky, that I needed a face to face before proceeding."

"What did he say?" She took out her phone and pulled up a strange looking text message dated this morning. I read it aloud.

"Delay impossible. Terminate by 8 PM tomorrow. Go to ghost and await further instructions." I felt sick reading it. "What does 'Go to ghost' mean?"

"That's what they say for getting rid of anything that shows we existed and then going far away from the scene. In this case it's supposed to be Montevideo." She took her phone back and began typing.

"Are you replying to that message?"

"I'm not. I'm trying to get ahold of Anna." She stared at the screen for a while. We didn't talk, but she did lean over and kiss me after a minute. I went with it slowly, and for a while we were like teens necking in a car for the first time just happy to be doing it. That didn't last and I pulled her to me making her phone hit the rug with a thud.

"Being alive is not so terrible sometimes." She said that before we stopped talking. It probably seems strange or stupid, but none of the new information about Nicki, now that it was out in the open, changed anything for me. On the contrary, I was more voracious for her than before, and she seemed to be as well tearing my shirt off without paying much attention to the buttons. She bit me several times as if intending to draw blood. Although my mouth was filled with every inch of her that I could get to, I did manage to proclaim my love to her again. She grabbed a fistful of my hair pulling my head back so she could feast on my throat like a vampire.

"Well, it appears that I love you too, you poor boy." She moved her head up until we were nose to nose and spoke into my mouth. "You have to try to keep loving me no matter what 'cause, believe me, there are gonna be some 'matter whats' ahead of us."

"Always." We didn't discuss anything more. It was our best night; I hope it wasn't our last night.

Chapter 33

BEN FORD

I think I managed to sleep for a few hours that night, but it was not deep. The very presence of Nicki, of course, made me want to remain conscious every second, but a sensation that I had felt since I was a child was especially prominent that night. Life has always seemed temporary to me. Even though everyone knows that to be true, for me each second that passes is a drop poured from a spigot that will soon run dry; every time I touched Nicki, I imagined it as the last time. I had read some poet who said that a woman had been "turned on the lathe of God for him," and when I said that to Nicki as we lay in each other's arms, she didn't laugh. Just as she started to reply there was a loud knock on the door.

"Damn!" She jumped up so quickly that she almost knocked me off the bed. Holding her gun in both hands, she walked toward the door.

"Yes?" She said this crouching to one side. I started dressing because it seemed better to not be naked whatever was going to happen.

"We need a meeting, boss lady." It was Suki, and she was not happy. Nicki still kept her body to one side of the door as she peered through the peephole. Nicki stepped away and threw on some clothes. When she opened the door, Suki entered followed by Max and Langston.

No one in the group seemed thrilled to be there, but Suki seemed barely able to control her anger as she walked around the room stopping to look at the view without really looking at it. The other two stayed by the door, and the silence was uncomfortable until Nicki broke it.

"You get some information?" Suki went straight to the mini bar and took out a bottle of Wild Turkey.

"I got some orders. Just as room service delivered the omelet that is still sitting in my room." She took a sip of bourbon. "Somebody thinks that you're not taking orders anymore. That somebody wants me to make sure that's not the case, that you aren't as Foxtrot Uniform as you've been acting."

"You know the order they are taking about?" Nicki was sitting next to me on the bed, her hand still resting on the gun that lay between us. She was looking at Suki, and her back was to the others. My head went back and forth.

"Deed I do, boss." Suki removed her Cardinals t-shirt slowly to reveal her grey sports bra with a bloodstain at the top from yesterday's killing. She also revealed the large handgun stuck in the waistband of her jeans. "And I need to know what you gonna do." The two women studied each other for a long time without saying a word. Max and Langston seemed concerned at the length of the silence, which made me think that I should say something. As I started to, Suki put a finger across her lips and shook her head.

"OK then. I'll do this." Nicki made a deliberate gesture to pull her hand away from the gun, sliding forward off the bed to come to rest on her knees on the floor. "You should know that I already texted Anna to tell her that she was in danger."

"Fuck you." Suki was more confused than angry by Nicki's announcement and by her kneeling.

"It's the wrong thing to do."

"We don't get to make that decision. Remember? That's why we're so special." She waved her hand in front of her crotch slightly touching the handle of the gun. I started feeling sick.

"Then you go do it then and get paid." Nicki said this in a very low voice. "But you do me first right here because I know that's part of the order." Suki snorted as she pulled the pistol out of her jeans and placed the silencer on it just as I had seen it in that basement.

"I could do it and never think about it again. You know that, right?"

"I know you could."

"What you boys think about this? You got something to say?" Suki addressed the men who still stood by the door, but her eyes never left Nicki.

"Fuck the orders." This came from Langston without much emotion. Max said, "Yeah" after a slight hesitation. Suki laughed, but still held the gun.

"Girl, have you fucked the whole team or are they just as dumb as you?" She ran her left hand through her hair and sighed. "I ought to execute this whole group and your dumb boyfriend and this fake prophet so I can be a big hero." She turned back to the mini bar. "But it seems that I am too stupid to do anything but wait to be terminated myself." Just at that moment Nicki's text went off. She picked up her phone.

"It's Anna. She's on the move." She came to her feet as she texted an answer. "I'll go get her myself, and you can all just say I was already gone when you came for me."

"You ain't goin' nowheres without me, my beauty." Suki was doing some accent that I couldn't place, but it got a laugh out of everyone else. "You boys in?" They were, and the whole group started to move together like a team. The others went back to their rooms with an intensity on their faces, but also a relief at going in some direction. Nicki put several clips into a large Gucci bag as she continued to text with Anna. At some point, she went in the bathroom and came out wearing a Mizzou sweatshirt. When Suki reentered the room, she did not knock.

"What about him?" Suki looked at me as if I were a stain on the rug. Nicki reached over and touched my cheek very gently.

"He does whatever he wants to do." She removed her hand. "He can get an Uber to the airport and go far away and never look back."

"Take that deal, civilian. We all screwed up and shit." Suki was wearing a black Sex Pistols sweatshirt that surprised me because it was pretty warm out. I was considering asking Nicki if we could talk for a minute, but I knew that was impossible. Actually, everything seemed impossible, and I was still thinking about throwing up. Nicki continued to look at her phone.

"Or he can come with us and secure Anna." Suki groaned as she pulled her hair into a tight ponytail. "She knows that he's with me and really wants to see him about something." For all of the dumbest reasons I was ecstatic about the opportunity to stay with them. I could not bear to walk away.

"That's very professional." Suki started stuffing things in another purse and made as if to clout me with it. "I just hope this Dare bitch has some magical powers because we may need them." She now checked her phone. "Car is ready."

We all left the room in a fast walk and single file with Suki in front and Nicki in back. The elevator was fast and contained an older man who was friendly and chatty. He was from Memphis, and right after breakfast, he and his wife and daughters and grandchildren were all going up in the Arch. We didn't say much in response as our minds were very far from imagining just enjoying a day without care.

Chapter 34

BEN FORD

Nicki, Suki and I took the SUV dropping Lang and Max a block away where for some reason they were meeting their Uber taking them back to get the bulletproof Escalade. Suki drove, and Nicki sat beside her texting while I took the backseat. It seemed that Anna, after getting Nicki's warning text, had ducked out of where she was having breakfast into yet another Uber and ditched her security team. She was heading to the Central West End or was probably already there.

"She said that she had some kind of premonition last night that this was about to happen, said she felt death was very close."

"That's great. Let's go hang out with her against orders." Suki banged on the steering wheel with the palm of her hand. "I told Max to bring the Kalashnikov. I have a premonition that will send a lot of people to heaven." She had popped a pill up in the hotel saying that she had not slept a wink the night before. I don't know what it was, but she seemed very awake.

"We won't be needing that, girl. We'll just pick her up and head for the hood. With Max and Lang in front of us it will be a piece of cake."

"I hate cake! You know they can track people real easy nowadays.

If they tipped off the wrong folks to where poor Anna is sitting all unprotected, we might walk into some deep shit." On highway 64 Suki changed lanes constantly, never wanting to be behind another car for more than two seconds. "You should have told her to meet us downtown. It would have been safer."

"You don't tell Anna what to do. She gets some feeling about what is right, and that's what she does." Some guy honked at us for pulling into his lane.

"Ain't that just great. Did it ever occur to you that in the grand scheme of the universe, we don't mean shit? Maybe Anna thinks that we would be acceptable sacrifices to her cause." She bumped Nicki's head with her elbow. "I think I'd rather be a live atheist than a dead believer. That's all I'm saying."

"Anna doesn't believe that there are any atheists. She thinks everyone has a god." I think I remember saying that just to remind them that I was there.

"Yeah, I'm glad to hear that." I still had the feeling that Suki could kill me and not think anything about it. "Why, exactly, do we have your lover boy in the backseat? Is that another of Anna's premonitions or some happy horseshit?"

"It is. She wants to talk to him right now in case something happens to her today." She reached around and put a hand on my knee. "She thinks there is something special about Ben." Suki laughed in a way I didn't like.

"Hey, boyfriend. You think you're in love with my homegirl? She's a heartbreaker. You know about that?"

"I've considered the possibility."

"Good thing you considered the possibility, special boy."

"Shut up and drive." There was anger in Nicki's voice, but also something else.

"Oh. I can do two things at once. Not like you though. You can do five things at once. I saw that video." She thought she was hilarious and caught my eyes in the rearview mirror. "Hey, lover. You know Nicki's real name?"

"Shut up." Nicki knew she wouldn't. I didn't say anything.

"What? She didn't tell you her name. Man, even pole dancers do that after you buy them two drinks." She reached her hand over the headrest toward my face. "I'm Susan, by the way, a former black ops girl soon to be unemployed and probably un-alive." We were on Forest Park Boulevard now coming up to Euclid. I put my hand on Nicki's shoulder.

"What's your name?" Nicki turned around with a look that was both amused and serious.

"Not that it means a hill of anything, but my birth name was Jane Wallington." Suki slapped her knee hard. "Since I am also unemployed now, all that secret crap doesn't mean anything."

"There you go, boyfriend. You can marry her now."

"Shut the fuck up, Susan, and get on the clock." We're almost there."

The last few block down Euclid were slow going with people who seemed unaccustomed to parallel parking trying to do it. As we got closer to Anna, the two women went silent, and their heads turned constantly from side to side looking for anything unusual. When a van stopped two cars in front of us to make some kind of delivery, Suki said something that I couldn't catch. Nicki turned around to me.

"You should get out here and walk slowly up to where she is. That will give us a chance to check things out." She spoke without emotion as if she were a firefighter telling me to leave a burning house. "If anything goes down, just get on your knees with your hands on your head."

"I'm going with you."

Nicki closed her eyes as the car eased forward. Suki squealed.

"Ok, hotshot, but if there's a problem of any sort, your punch and me don't surrender to nobody, no how." I was wondering exactly what I was doing there, but for some reason I was glad and not especially scared. I think there is a point where you get so used to being scared that you adapt to fear, or else go crazy. It is possible that I was crazy; I just leaned forward and kissed the back of Nicki's head. Although she jumped, it was not from the kiss.

"There she is." We had just crossed McPherson, and I could see Anna sitting at one of the outside tables at place called Dressel's. She was wearing a blue sundress and very dark sunglasses. Her dark hair was down and fell to her elbows, which might have been because she had tilted her head back to take in the sun. "Park the car just up the street and watch that side. Go to her and tell her we are leaving in five minutes." She said the first part to Suki and the second part to me before she got out of the car to stand by what used to be the old Balaban's, her hand inside the Gucci bag.

I walked up on Anna, still in her sun-worshipping reverie, wondering whether I should cough or say her name or sit down at the table where a third of a glass of red wine waited for her. While I hesitated, she raised her head and smiled at me.

"We have to stop meeting like this, Big Ben." She pointed to a chair. "Take a seat. I've ordered the yummy chips they have here, and it's a beautiful day that will never come again." As I sat down, she took my hand as she removed her sunglasses with a brisk flourish.

"We can't stay. Nicki thinks you are in danger." She smiled and put her eyes on me.

"So I heard." She took a sip of her wine. "Which makes the blue of the sky, this dear heat from a fire some 90 million miles away, the decent Malbec coating my tongue, your apparition here, so much more precious." Her gaze affected me.

"We have less than five minutes." I couldn't think of much else to say, and I found myself in awe of her again. No one I had ever met seemed to feel such an absolute pleasure in just existing.

"Then we need to use the time well." She smiled as if she never wasted a minute. She moved very close to me, making the waiter, who might have been coming to take my drink order, change direction to another table. "Will you do something for me if I ask you to do it?" In speaking those words, her voice changed its tone into some combination of love and protection: a mother's voice.

"Yes." I should have said "what?" I didn't and just waited for her to go on.

"I need you to go someplace and write down everything that has happened to you since you came to town. You will have to spend a whole month in absolute isolation at a house I own to allow you to understand all that you feel about this little sliver of your consciousness."

"I don't understand." She squeezed my hand.

"I know you don't, but you will understand after you go through it. Trust me." She raised my hand from the table and kissed it. "Do it. Let your words take you toward the incomprehensible. Not that it matters, but if you do this, I will write you a check for one million dollars just like some quiz show."

"I will." To be honest, the money made the decision for me, but I was also strangely proud in the way she was asking me to do it. I felt like I was in a daze, and when the server stopped by to set the potato chips on the table, she was too embarrassed by the obvious emotion on display to say anything. At the same time, Nicki came up behind Anna.

"My crew will be here in three minutes. You should just get up and get in in the Escalade when I come back." She turned around immediately as if the subject was not open to any discussion. Anna rolled her eyes.

"She's a bossy one, isn't she?" I did not reply. "Anyway, I have a little house way out in western Missouri in a very isolated spot. You'll have everything you need away from all of this craziness that I will soon be putting an end to."

"A whole month? Alone?" I was watching Nicki walk back toward the corner.

"Yep. Nicki will be with me on a real clean-up duty." She looked over her shoulder at her. "If she is meant for you, she will still be around." She finished her wine, and we looked at each other with a bargain sealed between us. Nicki broke the spell.

"Here it comes. Just get in the back when it stops." Anna sighed and placed a $50 bill under her wine glass. I turned around to see the Cadillac cross the intersection just as I heard Suki scream.

"That's not her!" Three men were running hard across Euclid wearing Halloween masks. One of them pulled a shotgun out of a cardboard box that fell to the street. Apparently, Suki's words confused them just long enough to delay their shooting at us. We were standing, and Nicki stepped between the gunmen and us. The next thing I knew the man holding the shotgun jerked in two directions as both women shot him at the same time.

"Stay behind me." Anna seemed to be moving toward the car that was almost in front of us, and Nicki wanted her to stay put. She fired several more times in rapid succession. Later, they explained that since the shotgun had been the greatest threat, they had shot him first. Then, they had both chosen the same person second, which was bad luck for him, but also for Nicki. The third gunman managed to fire a few times before he was cut down with at least one hitting Nicki in the chest and making her slam backward into Anna.

"Get in the car!" She had fallen across the table with one hand grabbing a chair. The Cadillac stopped and Max was suddenly next to me.

The car behind him must have slammed into reverse when the shooting started and smashed into a Mercedes. Our waitress, who had just come outside with a tray, started screaming.

"Pick her up!" Suki came up to our table with her back to us, her head swiveling constantly. Max and I carried Nicki to the car as Anna cradled her head.

"Brave girl, brave girl." She gave her a kiss on the cheek right before we placed her in the back seat as gently as we could. Somehow, we all got in. Suki, Nicki, and I were in the backseat with Anna and Max in front. Langston, according to some plan, had already left in the SUV. Suki snapped open the blade of a large pocketknife before we had gone 10 feet.

"You get elected, soldier?" Nicki gave her a pained grin.

"No, but I got nominated real good." Suki sliced open the Mizzou sweatshirt in one motion. Instead of the bloody mess I was dreading to see, there was a dark green thing that turned out to be a bulletproof vest. I was overjoyed.

"Then you're all right?" I think I said a number of things that were inappropriate for the moment. Suki punched my arm.

"Shut up and help me get this off." She started to pull the zipper very slowly while I held the fabric at the shoulder. Nicki winced. "Easy, girl. Your tits get flattened?"

"It's lower, I hope." Suki kept lowering the zipper as we turned onto Kingshighway.

"Yeah, I see. They still gonna be perky, beauty queen." There was blood flowing in a steady trickle to the right of her sternum. Suki placed a piece of the sweatshirt over the wound. "Press firmly, but not too hard on that, lover. A couple of those ribs might be cracked." I did as I was told while she started looking for a first-aid kit that Max said was under the seat. Holding Nicki like that was almost an embrace.

"We should go the other way, back to Barnes." That's the big hospital on Kingshighway." Suki laughed at the suggestion, and even Nicki smiled. She patted my cheek.

"Just keep the pressure on like that until the Asian finds a bandage. Don't worry. I bleed more than this when I shave my legs."

A lot happened in the next hour, but in my mind, it is almost totally a blur. I think my emotions were so strong that I could have had a nervous breakdown if I had not been so focused on just holding Nicki (I still cannot call her by that other name) and feeling her fierce heart continue to pump blood beneath my fingers.

At some point, Max pulled into an alley and switched the plates on the car just in case anyone had taken a picture with an iPhone. Langston called Suki and was told to head west on Highway 70. We followed him leaving Saint Louis behind, slicing through the suburbs until the signs for Jefferson City loomed. When we stopped at a gas station, Langston was already there waiting for us. Nicki moved my hand from her chest that was bandaged by then as we pulled up to the pump.

"You all go inside and get me the closest thing they have to an espresso while we have some words." Everyone, including Anna, left the car without a word. Max started pumping gas.

"Are you sure you don't need a doctor?" I put my hand below the wound on her bare abdomen. The gas pump ticked away and a country song from a car radio blared in the background.

"I'm fine, sugar." She kissed me on the forehead. "Listen here. We need to split up for a bunch of reasons. We got no protection anymore, and I don't know what kind of cameras they had back there."

"I'm staying with you." I knew that she had made up her mind, but I said that anyway. She shook her head and kissed me harder than I would have thought.

"You're gonna go do this thing for Anna. It may be crazy, but at least it will get you out of town for a good while."

"How do you know about that?"

"She texted that idea to me, and when she turned around and looked at me, I could tell that you agreed to do it. That right?"

"That was before this." I moved my hand over her wound without touching it. She ran her fingers through her hair.

"Here's what's gonna happen. Lang is driving you down to this house in the country somewhere where you're gonna do this crazy thing for Anna." I started to object, but she put a long finger against my lips. "You'll be safe there. Lang will put some stuff in the place so we can keep watch over you the whole time."

"I don't know." I had agreed to it, of course, and Anna was paying me a life-changing amount of money.

"I know." She ran her hand gently over my neck just as the pump shut off with a thunk. "Now give me a decent kiss without the hug and think about me up in the woods."

We kissed for a while before she gently broke it off. Somehow, I got out of the car with what was left of my mind made up. There was nothing else to do but walk across to where Langston had parked. From the front of the little store Anna, holding an ice cream cone, blew me a kiss. Suki stuck out her tongue. Lang and I rode all the way to Jackson County with only the sound of the Waze app occasionally breaking the silence. His good humor was gone; I was wondering if that had just been an act. I was trying not to think about what was happening, and my mind was too confused to form words.

Chapter 35

BEN FORD

I am finished. This morning I left a note to that effect for the guy who brings me supplies. Although I still have two days left, there is nothing more to tell. I have no idea when they will come for me, or what I have accomplished here. It seems strange that I haven't left this old house for almost a month. Once, I considered going for a walk, but decided against it because Langston hooked up some security equipment that he said made this place "a fortress," and I did not feel safe leaving. If there are cameras here, I hope Nicki has been watching.

A couple of things I think I should mention about my stay here. For one thing, I did not change any part of my mind about Nicki during this long retreat. If anything, my feelings have grown stronger; her feelings are hers to have. I just hope that my love can fill up her heart to the brim, but I will accept whatever happens. I am strong enough now.

This strength may be a direct result of writing this. Never before have I looked at my life so deliberately, and the consideration of what has happened, especially what occurred with Anna Dare, has changed my life. At first, the money and the opportunity to be safe were my only motivations. Both of those probably seem base, but I was a very different person a month ago. My thoughts about Anna were quite conflicted in the beginning. On the one hand, I wanted to believe that she was just another charlatan preaching a false prophecy for her own personal gain. On the other, it was difficult to dismiss what she was saying since my parents had written many of those words themselves.

As I was writing this story, something happened to me. At night, I read from *The Way*, paying particular attention to my mother's brief poems in the back of the book. At first, I read them for how they allowed me to hear the sound of her voice again, and in the silence of my lair her strength, her smile, her competence filled the void again and again. My father's voice was there as well calmly making the case for belief. Still, I came back to those poems feeling them tap against my heart with the joy of someone who has found something, something beautiful that she wanted to share.

Although it did not happen on one specific night, over time my mother's words effected a great change in me. It was as if her hand patted my back as I read. I felt a glow come over me, not from a physical sensation, but from a spiritual one. Slowly, I received something I can only call Grace, as I understand the word. I have felt that touch ever since.

So that happened. I have done what Anna Dare asked with a reward far beyond what she promised. I am a new person now, one who sees that light, knows the path toward it, and accepts the hardships that may arise as I travel The Way. Anna Dare is the One.

Chapter 36

YATES

"So that's the end? Anna Dare just implicated herself as an accessory after the fact in two triple homicides and sent me the confession? What in the wide world of sports is going on here?" Yates had been pacing or at least restlessly moving around the room for the last ten minutes. Ryan was already developing a plan to get control of Anna Dare. His whole future depended on the next two days.

"I will get this straightened out as soon as I am on the ground." He tried to appear calm and confident as if he could make all of this go away, at least for Yates.

"I hope you do better than my dumb brother who should have stayed a college professor living the theoretical life."

"Your brother is a brilliant man." Milla said this as a simple statement of fact, not as a contradiction though Ryan thought it was. Yates smiled at her in a way that implied that they would be making love very shortly, as soon as Ryan left.

"You are right. And my brother was right about the bulk of this." He took a drink of Pellegrino before summing things up. "People need to believe that whatever truth they live by emanates from the supernatural, handed to some human on top of a mountain, maybe, but still not of this world. I gave the magic to Anna Dare because she was an unknown natural actress, and the little book she believed in preached a gospel that worked for modern life." Ryan had not heard it described in just that way even though he had assumed it.

"And you thought your brother could control her?" Milla spoke in a flat tone, and Ryan wondered how many of the revelations of that day had been news to her. Not a scintilla of shock crossed her unlined face as they discussed the conspiracy that she was now a party to.

"Yes, and that was the great mistake. The woman has always been unhinged, believing in these voices she heard, but now she needs someone to put a few nails in her so she can be our girl again." He laughed and turned to Ryan. "I will have that spook, Peterson, meet you in Saint Louis like the song says. He can do many things that have to do with law enforcement because he is truly beyond good and evil as far as such things go. His girl, whatever her name is, was right about that."

Milla was sitting with her back against the arm of the couch, her knees bent to avoid contact with Yates' hip. He reached over and gently picked up her feet placing them on his lap duly proud in the way he possessed them. If he was intending to make Ryan jealous with the gesture, he succeeded.

"I just notified security that you will be leaving shortly." She turned to Yates who was running a finger across her instep. "Unless you have further instructions." The great man shook his head with a grin that implied that he was eager for him to leave.

"Just keep me up to date on everything."

"I will text you as soon as I am on the ground." Ryan said this just as he noticed that another person had entered the room even though he had heard no footsteps approaching. At the exact moment that he realized that the very short person was not a servant coming to clean up their dishes, he noticed a large gun in his hand. Yates saw this as well and seemed about to jump off the couch when the person froze him speaking in a voice that was harsh and female, but hardly feminine.

"Not a muscle moves that I don't ask you to flex." The attacker wore a skin-tight black outfit with some sort of ski mask over her face. "We are all alone in this big house, so anything can happen."

"How did you get in here?" Yates was more angry than scared just then. The woman laughed. Ryan thought that the gun she was holding was called an Uzi, and he felt his hands start to shake.

"I can't tell you how many times I heard some dumbshit say that exact thing to me. Usually it's the very last thing they say." Another figure entered the room, a big man carrying what appeared to be an assault rifle. Milla quickly removed her feet from Yates' lap and moved to stand up. Ryan, thinking she had just lost control out of fear, braced himself for the impending shots that would turn her white robe red and probably get all of them killed.

"Actually, I let them in through your emergency escape tunnel that no one else knows about." Yates said nothing, and his face was hard to read. Ryan felt as if he were on a plane that had begun losing altitude, and the pilot's voice on the PA had just turned into a scream.

"Ain't that some shit, Richie Rich? Yeah, you need to get the cleaning crew down to work on that tunnel. It's real nasty in there."

"Schedule." The other gunman said this. Suki (Ryan assumed it was Suki) pulled out some handcuffs from a leather bag that hung over her shoulder.

"Ok, boys. Move over there really slow." She pointed to the large iron sculpture in the hallway. It looked like old rusty farm equipment that had been welded together to become a scarecrow without a head. In a moment they were on the floor, each handcuffed to one of the legs.

"He still has his phone." Milla offered that information as she pulled out a pair of jeans and a t-shirt from a cubbyhole next to the hot tub. She dropped her robe to the floor and was naked for a few seconds before she dressed. Ryan was too scared to care. Suki ran her hands over Yates as he sat on the floor.

"Let me check this out. Oops, that's the wrong thing. Yeah, here we go." She fished out the phone from the pocket of his robe tossing it toward the couch, but missing it with a clatter. Yates turned to Milla as she was pulling on her running shoes.

"You are finished, girl." Although Yates was probably going to say more, Suki interrupted him with a sudden, brutal punch to his solar plexus. She grabbed him by the hair with her gloved fingers as he gasped for air.

"That's just it, *Baichi*. You ain't finishing nothing. Anna sent you that little bedtime story, and then she sent us to show you that you no longer rule here." Her mask was very close to his nose, and Yates looked afraid for the first time. Suki was very angry as she went on, almost out of control. "You see money ain't all that all the time. Your girlfriend here takes your money, but she loves Anna Dare in a real big way. So she did all this, sent everybody out of the house, gave us the combination to the tunnel, kept your mind on her hot yoga body. She did it because Anna asked her to."

"But why?" Yates was having trouble getting the words out. "I support Anna. I made Anna who she is." Suki laughed.

"You don't get what's happening here. You never made Anna. She told me to tell you that, by the way." She opened the little satchel again. "You come after her in some legal way, and all your crimes come out in the open. If you go the other way, she has us now, the people you never want to see again the rest of your life." She was now holding a different, smaller pistol, which she fired, into Yates' chest with only the slightest whisper of a sound. He convulsed in agony.

"No, wait." Ryan started pulling the handcuffs as if he might free himself.

"Shut up, lawyer-face. It's just a tranquilizer." She turned the gun toward him. "Sweet dreams."

He heard the same little pop just before he felt as if a screwdriver had been pushed into his chest. Ryan's heart seemed to go immediately in reverse as it drained the blood away from his brain. Sinking away from the room and the dark figure standing over him, he saw Milla checking her hair in the mirror just above where he was lying.

Chapter 37

STEVEN YATES

After Anna parted ways with him, Steven Yates spent the first several weeks in a mild alcohol and sedative induced coma speaking to no one else in the world and not leaving his house even once. In the middle of the third week, he began contemplating suicide, and a few days later with the ever-helpful internet, he developed a painless and foolproof plan. The heavy plastic bag and the old bottle of painkillers waited grimly on his nightstand. The only reason he had not gone through with it was because he believed that he deserved to suffer for as long as he could endure it. He had failed his brother, the Messiah Project, his own beliefs, but, for some strange reason, the loss of Anna was the worst of it.

Anna had not actually dismissed Steven; she had simply texted him to vacate the premises of her house along with everyone else "to allow new security measures to be put in place." The language did not sound like her, but she never responded to any of his texts on the matter. After a day of waiting, he cleared everyone out and went to his house in Clayton to see what would happen. She never texted again or responded.

Once upon a time, he had been proud of his stately two-story home with its circle drive in front in an exclusive Saint Louis neighborhood, but now it seemed not just empty (he had only spent a few weeks there since moving in with Anna), but devoid of any life whatsoever. It even had a smell to it that, to be sure, could have been from his exclusive diet of Campbell's Chunky soup and the empty cans that he had allowed to accumulate in one corner of the kitchen as if throwing them in the trash would be pointless. His brother had helped him buy the house with a gift of money for his 50th birthday, a gift that for an absurdly rich man was like the tip most people would give a good waiter. His brother had called him only twice after things went wrong with Anna, and he could tell from the curtness in his voice that he no longer considered him a part of the project. Robert had almost hung up on him the second time out of exasperation. A few minutes later, Steven received a call from Peterson as if his brother had delegated the responsibility to him.

"Are you able to speak?" Peterson was all business as usual. He had only spoken to him a few times, and he always implied that he had only a few minutes left to prevent a disaster somewhere. Robert must have told him that his sanity was in question.

"I am all alone if that is what you mean." He wanted to be brisk with Peterson, which was impossible. He spoke before he finished his sentence.

"What is the current status of Anna Dare?"

"Sorry. I don't think I am the guy to help you with that." Steven wondered whether Peterson was using some interrogation technique trying to determine if he had told his brother the truth about having no contact with Anna. It bothered him, and he decided to let his temper go. "Why don't you ask one of the serial killers in your employ? I'm sure they are great at finding people." He heard Peterson take a deep breath.

"You should hope that they don't try to find you, my friend."

"Don't threaten me, you fuck." He was taking pleasure in allowing his despair to become anger. "Your crack team wasn't all it was cracked up to be, was it?" Peterson responded with the briefest chuckle, the most annoying response possible, as if nothing Yates could say could ever affect him.

"You are dealing with a world with which you are at an extreme disadvantage, Professor Yates." He used the word "professor" as if it were a pejorative. 'If you do hear from Anna Dare, contact me at this number. It is imperative that I meet with her."

"And kill her?" Peterson sighed.

"I have no interest in killing Anna. Your brother and some of his powerful friends tried to go around me after they panicked about her exposing them. They also have felt the sting of meddling with things they know nothing about." He hesitated. "By the way, professor, you almost got Anna killed by leaving her unprotected and telling people where she was."

"I didn't leave her unprotected. She took off on her own after she had some sort of premonition or at least that was what she texted me. She left her bodyguards."

"And told you where she was going?"

"Yes, she did, but I didn't tell anyone except the security team." He realized what he was saying. "Maybe one of them…"

"Yes, that could be what happened. I am fairly sure at least one of them was a spy for various people, mostly for his own gain. Not really your fault." Peterson was trying to be some version of good cop now or maybe it was something else. If there was a spy, his brother had put him there to make sure that he had control over everything as he always did. But it had not worked out as he thought; nothing had, nothing except Anna.

"I am a complete fool." Steven had never imagined that he could say those words with such conviction. Now they fit perfectly in his mouth.

Peterson either did not hear, or chose to ignore, his confession. He seemed anxious to end the call.

"The important thing now is for you to get me that meeting with Anna to allow me to straighten things out." He waited for a response and received none. "Just tell her that the meeting is with Raymond Peterson. She will take it."

Yates did not ask him why that would be so, and for a long while he stared at the phone without moving. He tried Anna's old cell number, but it was no longer working. Eventually, he reread the article from the Hemlock Society on his IPad, checked the expiration date of the oxycodone pills on his nightstand, and made a decision. He would drive to Ferguson tomorrow and make one last attempt to talk with Anna, if for no other reason than to apologize to her. Maybe one of the killers would be there and end his life for him. He supposed that would be easier than doing it himself.

The next morning he woke up and made a list of people that he should call on his last day, a few old colleagues, his favorite niece, a woman he was once engaged to. His brother was not on that list. He had just opened what was, appropriately, his last can of Chunky Soup when three sharp knocks sounded on his front door two seconds apart. When he looked out the peephole, a young woman wearing huge dark sunglasses stared back at him smiling. With a second look he realized it was the reporter Jill whatever her name was, the one Anna had made famous on one of her whims. In his current state of mind, he opened the door, not caring whether someone lurked out of view behind his hydrangeas. Jill wore faded black jeans and a white Clash t-shirt and carried a very large handbag. She was alone.

"Good morning, Professor Yates." She removed her sunglasses to reveal her blue eyes as if she were performing a magic trick as she looked around. "Nice house. My parents live only a few blocks from here."

"That's very interesting. Can I help you?"

"I would like to help you if I can, Professor." He realized that he had not combed his hair yet that morning and probably looked as if he needed help. She took him up on his offer of a glass of water and followed him into the kitchen.

"Was it hard to find me?" He spent some time looking for an appropriate, relatively clean glass while she perched on one of the retro bar stools that surrounded his kitchen island.

"Not really. Anna told me you would be here." She placed the heavy bag next to her, and he wondered if it contained a recording device of some kind.

"So you are still in touch with Anna?" He hoped that he didn't sound sad, but assumed he did. He was sad.

"Yes. We have been together constantly this last week." She flipped some of her dark red hair over her shoulder. Steven placed the ice water in front of her.

"So what was it exactly with you and Anna? Were you romantically involved with each other?" He was genuinely curious and no longer cared what she might think about the question. In the beginning of their relationship, Steven had assumed that he and Anna would become lovers. She was still quite attractive and seemed to possess some interest in sex. When that did not happen, despite their almost constant intimate contact, he supposed that her interests were probably not heterosexual. Jill laughed.

"I can see where you might be confused because I do love Anna more than I have loved anyone." She took a drink of her water and seemed more exhilarated than embarrassed at her revelation. "Wow! Is that like the meme for sad bachelors?" Jill pointed at the just opened can of Chunky Soup on the far end of the island. "Do you at least put it in a bowl?"

"Ms. Devereaux, if you are looking for a quote from me about some piece of investigative journalism, I am afraid I will have to disappoint you." He leaned in the direction of the front door hoping she would just leave. She stayed put.

"Oh, I don't need much from you about your rich brother fixing the lottery or using his power to control the mechanizations of the brain we call the internet. No, that story is out there, and your brother's buddies have already managed to make it into fake news. Even your full confession could not resurrect it." She blinked a few times as if trying to remind him that her eyes were still amazing.

"Then what do you want from me?" She reached into her bag and pulled out a rather large document that she tossed on the island in front of him.

"Anna sends you this. You need to read it."

"What is it?" He picked up the package. The top page was blank except for a phone number scrawled in the lower left hand corner.

"It is a sort of diary, an account of recent events by one Benjamin Ford. You remember him?"

"I don't care about him. I am done with all of this, and, moreover, the world is done with me." When his hand came down hard on the document with a violent slap, he wondered if Jill might be afraid. She was a young woman all alone in a house with a desperate, angry man, but she remained icily calm.

"The world may be done with you, but Anna, for some reason believes that you may have something left to give." She drained her remaining water in a single gulp. She slid off the bar stool shaking her head at the pile of dishes in the sink.

"What does she want?"

"Just read this and call that number afterward if you want to be with Anna again." She put on her sunglasses and moved to exit the kitchen.

"And she also would probably want you to clean up this dump before the bugs take over, but that's just my guess." She left shutting the front door loudly.

Steven remained in the kitchen staring at the document. With some trepidation, he finally opened it. When he read the first words, "by the time anyone reads this, I will probably be dead," a flood of tears raced to his eyes. He felt an odd mixture of emotions, the joy of having some reason to live mixed with the fear of losing that reason. He picked up the document and began reading.

Chapter 38

NICKI

One surprising consequence of being around Anna Dare night and day, as Nicki had for the last month, was to have developed an acute awareness of her life, every second of it. Even the most mundane activity was poignant if it was a step on The Way because it was a step you were supposed to take. As she walked down the stairs in Anna's house in the Ozarks, the rough boards had a primitive feel against her bare feet. At the bottom, she rose briefly on her toes stretching her arms above her head in a delightful validation of her sinews. Nicki wore a black t-shirt and cutoff olive drab combat pants with the Kel-Tec PMR-30, the gun that had not left her side in a month, in the pocket pressing snugly against her thigh.

"Good morning, chief." Langston was checking the various security monitors while eating a four-egg omelet directly from a skillet. Nicki pulled the fork from his hands and took a bite that was heavy with onion.

"Morning. We all good?" She thought that now that Ben was staying here, Lang needed to start wearing pants, and she made a mental note to tell him later. At least his Marine t-shirt covered most of his scrotum.

"Yeah, nobody getting in here without me knowing about it." He continued fiddling with some dials. "A deer tripped an alarm early this morning and interrupted my beauty sleep. That seems to happen every dang day, so I might need to adjust some of these settings."

"Leave it tight. You are pretty enough already." She stared at the monitors.

"Ben sleeping in?"

"He is dead to the world." Nicki said nothing more, and Lang grinned in acknowledgement of how strenuous their reunion must have been.

"You going for a run before it gets hot?" He offered her some more omelet, but she shook her head.

"In a minute. I just came down to see if there was anything going on." She looked at the monitor that featured the black Range Rover sitting at the entrance to their gravel road. The two security guards in the car, from the same outfit she had hired in Ferguson, had mostly lived up to her expectations.

"Just let me know when you leave." He went back to his equipment and his breakfast, but still wanted to talk. "Why do you think Anna picked him up without you after that month?"

"She had Suki and Max, and she wanted us to set up security on this place."

"They were together almost a whole week in Montana." He thought a minute. "It just seems strange."

"Anna just does stuff. You know that." She was trying not to act as if the additional week had bothered her, but it had. "Besides, she wanted to talk to him about this thing he wrote." Lang had been running a test on one of the systems and seemed pleased with the results.

"Yeah. I don't get that either. You get to read it yet?"

"Not yet, but he has a copy with him." Lang gave her a teasing look that meant that he had read it.

"You'll get around to it soon, I expect." He resumed eating. "Hey, is he calling you Jane now? And you calling him Tarzan?"

"You're talking to Suki too much. Both of you are gonna be old ladies in no time if you keep up the jabbering." He laughed in that big way throwing his head back to reveal his boxer shorts, which featured tiny pictures of the old cartoon characters, Boris and Natasha.

"Just let me know Janey." She fingered him without turning around and that broke him up again. He was still at it when she climbed back to the second floor.

The big mirror at the top of the stairs was mounted to make it impossible to avoid her somewhat disheveled reflection, and, as she had been trained, she made some mental notes of the parts that needed improvement. When she first met Peterson, he held her firmly by the shoulders and made her stare at a lighted, unforgiving mirror. In his deep voice, he ordered her to change her expression to evince different emotional states as he spoke them. He intoned the words "amused, intrigued, aroused, innocent, libidinous (he wanted to see if she knew what that meant), brazen, arrogant, submissive." After he exhausted many possibilities, Peterson tapped lightly on her back.

"Perfect. The best I have ever witnessed." She was still looking in the mirror at her now blank expression.

"So what do I win? Does this mean I'm hired?"

"It is up to you, but if you agree to undergo the training, and only if you agree to every bit of it, I can make you into the greatest weapon in my arsenal. You will be able to go anywhere, have intelligence given to you on a platter, and make the most loyal followers betray their beliefs. All you have to do is tell me this is what you want to become."

She had agreed to everything he asked without hesitation and became just the thing he wanted. Like the Circe of her codename, she easily turned men, and a few women, into swine who did her bidding. As opposed to a normal honey trap operative, she was also capable of snapping the necks of those whose usefulness she had exhausted. She reveled in this power, and it fulfilled all of her desires to flourish outside the rules of society. Looking at her confused expression in the mirror, Nicki wondered whether she could give that up. Even though she had told Peterson she was quitting, he refused to accept her resignation. She wondered if he knew something about her that even Anna did not know. She hoped not.

As she entered the master bedroom where Ben slept, one arm covering his face to block the light seeping in through the closed blinds, she did not make a sound. Even sitting on the bed did nothing to rouse him. Anna Dare had meticulously decorated the room to become the most feminine place she had ever slept in. The walls were the lightest shade of pink with roses of that exact same hue dotting the diaphanous white drapes. The big chaise was silver sateen. Of course, there was a huge king bed that was topped with a fluffy pale blue comforter and had sheets with some astronomical thread count. Nicki slowly tugged down the sheet from around his waist to both gently wake him and to study his pale nakedness at her leisure. Although he had been indoors too much lately, those many months of moving furniture had given him a broad chest and wide shoulders. He moved his arm slightly, and she made a mental note to get him to a barber who could clean up the dark, thick hair that wafted over his ears. It was impossible for her to believe she was having such thoughts.

In the beginning, Ben was just another assignment, a person she needed to trust her until she could get information from him, but something had gone wrong. Her training made most men exceptionally easy to read, easy to seduce, easy to discard. She had given herself to Ben with abandon because she could tell that no woman ever had. Although that surely had been an effective strategy, a complication had arisen, one that still eluded her.

"Hey, gorgeous girl." Ben opened his eyes and put his hand on her bare thigh, his touch both light and firm. That odd mixture was some of the strange part about him. Most young men with an abundance of hormones and a low amount of success in life had, she found, a surplus of anger that easily turned to cruelty. Nicki had read the anger correctly, but there was almost no cruelty in Ben. Although sexually he wanted to ravish her, he seemed incapable of causing pain. She thought that misreading of his nature had thrown her off her game, but Anna just laughed at that explanation and punched her on the arm. "You are not the master of your heart forever, my dear girl."

"Hey, sleepy." Nicki brushed her hand over his already turgid penis. "At least somebody's awake."

"Awake and hungry for life." Ben had a new way of speaking since she had last seen him. She noticed it immediately when she picked him up at the airport in St. Louis. He was not as hesitant as before, more confidant of his right to things in the world.

"So how was it up in Montana with Anna?" They had not had much time for talking about it the previous evening.

"It was beautiful what I got to see of it. Most of the time Anna wanted me around as she was reading my whatever it was that I wrote."

"Did she pay you that money she said she would?" He nodded. "Yay! You're a rich man no matter what else happens."

"I am a rich man in ways I never imagined." He kissed her hand.

"So is that all you did day and night up there with Suki and Max standing guard?"

"Max and I hiked some, and Suki mostly complained about the food. At night Anna, Jill and I played board games. She loves Monopoly." Nicki stood up.

"Jill Devereaux was up there, um hmm. How did that go with your not having any for a month?" Nicki was more upset that Anna had not told her about Jill; she wasn't sure about her.

"Nothing like that is definitely going to happen ever. But it is interesting to see that you care, my free spirit." He pulled her gently back to the bed. "She was there to make suggestions about what parts of my writing should be leaked to the internet."

"That Jill is so smart." Nicki did not like anything she was feeling and decided to focus on something else. "She wants to leak your story out to the world? Isn't that a problem for Anna?"

"It could be, but she doesn't care about problems. I don't either. You should read it tonight or as soon as you can." He was different all right. Maybe from being a hermit after all that violence or maybe from spending a week with Anna. She could give you real courage, not burying your fears as Nicki had always done, but not having them. Anna seemed to have done this with Ben.

"You feeling pretty good about yourself, ain't you?" His hands were roaming freely over her.

"How about a walk, maybe? I'm a little out of shape from being cooped up for a month. All I could do was pushups and dips while holding ten copies of The Way."

"That seemed to work pretty well for you." She ran her hand over his chest. "We can take a walk then. Unfortunately, this would require you to get out of bed and put some clothes on." He grabbed her hand and kissed it.

"I feel like I'm on my honeymoon." He gently bit her shoulder. "And it's not a bad feeling at all."

"Uh-huh. What you want for breakfast, honeymooner? Lang can make almost anything if he doesn't eat it first."

"Those steaks were great last night, especially after all the frozen crap I've been eating, but I think I'll wait until after the walk." He leaned forward to kiss her. "On the other hand, there are forms of indoor exercise that burn many calories and even use all of the major muscle groups." She stood up.

"Later, sex addict of my heart. I need some fresh air in my lungs, and you need to see some of the scenery. You have been too cooped up." She punched his bare leg that stretched out to try to hook around her waist. "I'll be waiting for you downstairs so you can concentrate." She left him in the big bed grinning at all his luck.

Nicki waited at the bottom of the stairs wondering where this was all going. More than that, she wondered where she wanted it to go. Even as a very young girl, the thought of falling in love had repulsed her after witnessing what love had done to her mother. The poor woman gave herself away to any man who took the slightest interest in her and willingly suffered whatever abuses they inflicted upon her (and on Nicki before she could defend herself). She always found another man until one of them beat her to death before blowing out what passed for his brains. Nicki was in the Navy already when it happened, and she didn't even take leave to go to whatever hick town her mother was living in to bury her.

"Let's go commune with nature." Ben was wearing the new clothes she had bought for him (Anna had bought) and looked like some rich kid who wore J. Crew to go hiking. She yelled to Lang in the kitchen that they were on their way out. A drone rose slowly behind them as they left the yard.

"He's got eyes on us. That's good, but I guess we can't get too freaky in the woods." She pointed at the little craft hovering low just above the trees. "Unless we want to give our boy a free show." They both waved at the drone. The path they were on dove straight into the woods as the big lake pushed through every gap to expose its sun-drenched azure surface. Anna's house was on the isolated south side of the lake, and there were no houses close.

"Does Anna have a boat here?" Ben was keeping up pretty well at the brisk pace she was setting.

"She has two, a little john boat and a pontoon boat. Nothing fancy."

"Maybe we should take one out this afternoon. It is such a great day." She nodded without comment.

Ben really had no idea the exact situation he was in which she found both endearing and annoying. Anna had sent Suki and Max to California to do some dangerous things, things that could have major repercussions for all of them, and she didn't think he was ready for any more violence. She didn't know if he was ready for many things even if he claimed to be. As he took her hand, she was not sure.

"I have to do something with Anna tomorrow night. It might be a rough thing." She wanted to bring him down to earth.

"The meeting with Peterson, your old boss?"

"You know everything, don't you?"

"Anna texted me last night. She is not worried about it." They were exiting the thick trees with the calm water in front of them stretching to the horizon. She let go of his hand that had been grasping hers since they started.

"You know what I am, right? I don't think you do." He stared out at the lake as he replied.

"I know that you have done some extreme things, but Anna would say…"

"I know what Anna says about starting a new life. I read the book." She waited until he turned to look at her. "But I don't think I can ever do normal. The regular world is like another planet to me."

"Yes, I get that about you. I also know that I have the strength not to care what you need to do or want to do as long as you are in my life." He went back to looking at the lake before removing his shoes and socks.

"Really?" So Anna thinks she knows I have changed?"

"Anna thinks you believe you have changed, and that is the only thing that matters. Her opinion and the world's opinion mean nothing." Nikki stared at him in silence, as the birds filled the air with calls for food and mates. Ben kissed her forehead and spoke again.

"You know what we could do? We could swim out there until I am exhausted and can't take another stroke. Then you could drag me back in some Navy Seal life-saving technique you must have learned. C'mon, let's skinny dip and give Lang a show."

"I might drown your ass."

"I want to put myself in your hands." He was naked now and walked right into the lake where he began a sort of dog paddle that she doubted he would be able to sustain for long. She undressed quickly keeping her back to the hovering drone, setting her gun underneath her clothes. In the water, she went into the combat sidestroke that she knew would catch him easily. Nicki wondered why she was doing this, but she was strangely happy that she didn't care.

Chapter 39

PETERSON

Peterson had never been in Saint Louis before except to change planes back in the day when it was the TWA hub. Since then, the city had developed a bad reputation for violent crime, and as he drove through the downtown area on a night that the Cardinals were not in town it was as deserted as one of those fake cities in China. With the reassuring feel of his Glock 19 under his sport coat, he was not especially worried about carjackers, and there were few people who looked even vaguely threatening. It was still light out when he handed the keys to the valet, a young man who aroused no suspicions.

Al's Steakhouse, just a short walk from the Mississippi River, had the look and sounds of a place straight out of the early 60s. There was a greeter in evening clothes and Sinatra crooned softly from speakers in the ceiling. A mural depicted the riverfront in the 19th century when steamboat traffic crowded the water making Saint Louis an economic force to be reckoned with. After the maître d found his reservation under "Dare," he gave Peterson a brief look, but led him to his table without a word. Out of habit, he took the seat facing the front door, and ordered a Widow Jane neat from the attentive waiter.

"There is another person in your party, sir?" The waiter asked this by way of being thorough as the bus boy rushed up to fill water glasses.

"Yes. I am waiting for Anna Dare."

"Very good, sir." He got the reaction he wanted as the busboy's hand shook a little as he poured the water in anticipation of seeing a celebrity. It was a silly thing to do, but he felt foolish being there at all.

He should never have involved himself with any of this. The passion of all those impossibly rich men out to save the world or at least the world they wanted to preserve, had convinced him to participate in their dumb little scheme. Although he was aware that his supposed boss (he never acknowledged the authority of these appointed men) was a supporter and that he was absolutely insulating him from culpability, it was their flattery of his ability to do impossible things that had convinced him to make the poor decision to join them. He knew that now, but it made no difference at this point. His duty was to clean it up and set things right as he always did.

"There she is." He said this as the waiter set his drink down lightly on the table. The man's eyes followed Peterson's pointed finger to where Anna Dare stood at the front door.

She did not see him, but Nicki, who entered right behind her, clearly did although she did not change her firm expression one iota. She wore a blue tailored suit and carried a large bag over her shoulder that he assumed contained all of the firepower she thought she might need for the evening. She scanned the room thoroughly before taking a seat at the bar. Anna Dare surveyed the restaurant as well as she waited for the maître d to seat another couple, but she did it as a painter might, drinking in every detail for future reference. Walking to the table, she seemed unaware of the stares and sudden whispers from the other diners who were realizing that a celebrity was in their midst. She wore a white tunic dress that he thought was a little too short for a woman her age, especially one desiring to be taken seriously as a religious leader. Her hair, also too long for someone her age, poured forth from her head in a dark mass of natural curliness. He stood up as she reached the table.

"Ray! How lovely to see you again. How long has it been?" His first name was indeed Raymond, but no one else had ever called him "Ray" other than Anna. When he took her hand in greeting, he felt her firm grip, one that was both loving and possessive. He wondered if she did that with everyone now.

"More than a few years and under quite different circumstances." When she sat down, the waiter pushed her chair in as if he was performing a ritual. He took her drink order with a head bowed more than normal.

"Yes, you were quite the man of mystery back all those years ago, and I suppose you still are." She waited until they were alone to continue. "What was the name of that ridiculously handsome banker I was seeing back then in New York? I was ever so shocked when you approached me with the news that he was laundering money for some unsavory characters." Peterson could see why she had done so well in the role of prophet. The tone of her voice, her very demeanor, implied that of a powerful person who focused completely on whomever she was with.

"Terrorists to be exact." He used his most professional voice to respond.

"Yes, and I cooperated so fully to get whatever it was you needed to put them away that you and I became involved for more than a bit of carnal fun at that safe house in, where was it?"

"Brussels." She was flirting with him, and he began to analyze why she would.

"That's right, but I don't remember seeing much of the city." The waiter brought her the Malbec she had ordered. Peterson could not tell exactly what Anna was up to, but he kept an eye on Nicki at the bar.

He saw an older man approach her, probably to offer to buy her a drink, and she waved her left hand at him that must have sported a fake wedding ring. Her eyes never left their table.

"Nicki seems upset." He smiled in her direction. She took a drink of what was probably club soda without reacting. Anna sipped her wine.

"She thinks that you want me dead or at least are willing to do that job for some other people who want me dead." There was a basket of rolls on the table and she spent some time finding the one that she wanted. "She does not believe that someone else used your secret communications system to tell her to do me in." Peterson watched her butter the length of the croissant she had chosen before replying.

"It was a momentary glitch in the command structure." She looked at him as if he was speaking down to her, and she was more amused than angry. He softened his tone slightly. "I could have easily regained control and assured your safety if you had not done that foolish business with Yates a few days ago." He touched her hand that was not holding the croissant.

"Yates needed to be reminded that he does not control everything in the world."

"The Asian girl is dangerous without a firm hand controlling her. She could have made some very bad decisions in that situation." He pressed slightly on her finger that rested on the table.

"We all could." She brought back her smile. "So now Yates has reiterated his order, I suppose. He wants you to rid him of this crazy woman." She did not react to his touch, but did not move her hand either. Peterson thought that was a good sign.

"Anna, people, very powerful people do believe that you have become irrational to the point of being dangerous." He gently massaged her index finger.

"And you have come here to rein me in by threatening me?" She took a bite and made a face of ecstasy that was so genuine that he almost laughed, but knew he had to remain serious. She was clearly unstable.

"I am here to help you and find a way to get you out of this toxic situation before someone hurts you." She slid her hand out from under his to pick up her napkin and dab her lips. "I don't know if you are aware of it, but it was my influence with local authorities that cleaned up Nicki's messes without implicating you."

"My hero." Someone at another table was trying to take a surreptitious photo of them. When she saw Peterson instinctively cover his face with his hand, she turned around and smiled at the young woman who was embarrassed, but pleased. Anna kept the smile on her face. "Tell me, Ray dear, did all those rich men know that we had a past when they selected me to be the face of their little cult?"

"No, they did not." He decided to let her express herself somewhat so that it would be easier for her to think that accepting his help was a choice that she could make of her own volition instead of an ultimatum from him.

"You didn't tell them?"

"It seemed like a fact they did not need to know." She took another bite of her croissant with the same relish as before. He wondered whether there was another in the basket.

"But you remembered me, didn't you?"

"When I saw your photo in the file, yes."

"Did you think they had made a good choice?"

"I did." He liked that she was seeking his approval now, a sure sign that the woman was very afraid. This was going much easier than he had anticipated. She wanted his protection, and was not above bringing up their old love affair to get it. "You always had a certain charisma that drew people to you, made them agree with what you were saying even if they didn't understand quite what it was." She laughed at that.

"That's all it took to charm you, dear boy?" He ignored that comment to end her flirtation and press his point.

"But I also thought that you knew how to follow orders without questioning them because that is the only way that people in extreme situations have a chance of surviving. Many people want to kill you, Anna. You know that you need my protection right now as much as you did back in Brussels." The waiter approached their table pushing a little cart. Anna popped the last bit of croissant in her mouth.

"Times change." Her mouth was full as she said this.

Al's Steakhouse had no written menus. The cart that pulled up next to their table contained the various raw cuts of steak and seafood that were available that evening which the waiter described in detail. When he reached the Chateaubriand, mentioning that it was for two, Anna tapped her nose and winked at Peterson. They ordered that with two Caesar salads and something called ideal potatoes, which she wanted to share as well. He agreed, but he was growing tired of being agreeable.

"Anna, you need my guidance." He said this as soon as the cheerful waiter left. "This business with getting the Ford boy to hide out for a month and put his very dangerous thoughts on paper was a great mistake. What the hell were you thinking?" She raised one eyebrow.

"I don't always think about every detail as you do." She stared into his eyes as if she could look straight through his retina into his cerebrum. He thought it a good trick that must have worked on many people. "Sometimes I just know what is supposed to be done."

"Is that so? Well, now that you have it and I have it, too, what do you plan to do with it?" He saw Nicki shift in her seat, and he wondered if she could read lips at this distance.

"I don't intend to do anything with it." The waiter was returning with a different cart to prepare their Caesar salads tableside as he had said. The process transfixed Anna as if she were a student in cooking class. Peterson thought about the night he ended their affair many years ago. She had accepted his usual litany of reasons without complaint, in the way an experienced woman would, and he had appreciated that at the time. Only at their final tryst had she mentioned her connection with some deity that gave her life purpose and made any terrible circumstances (suffering, failure, loss) bearable. At the time, he assumed that she had simply misread Heidegger or Buber or some other old man, whose dusty thoughts she had converted into revelation. Now they were involved in a different assignation, but he still desired to make her bow to his thinking, even if, once again, she needed to find strength in her vision of some god. They ate their salads, which had much more than a hint of anchovy, in silence until she spoke again.

"You, on the other hand, could put Ben's memoir, or select parts of it, out on the dark web where it would become a mystery and a testimonial of The Way changing a life."

"What would be the point of that?" He finished his bourbon and thought he should have ordered a glass of wine.

"Hard to say, but I have a feeling that Ben may be the one to keep things going after I no longer can. I would ask you to trust me." She savored a drink of her red wine. "Then I will entertain any and all suggestions that you and your powerful cabal might have to correct my erratic behavior." Setting down her wine glass, Anna took his hand again, raised it to her lips, and kissed it briefly.

"I suppose I can put an edited version out there." Some part of the group would enjoy making people see Ford's story as yet another sign of Anna Dare's divinity; such people enjoyed the feeling that they could control the truth that rolled through cyberspace. They ordered more wine, and he felt that he had mostly solved the problem. He looked at her now and smiled. These delusions she had and her passion for them could still be useful, until they no longer were.

"So any other instructions from my handler before the Chateaubriand arrives?" Peterson looked down at his hand and saw the pale stain of her lipstick.

"Yates, Stephen Yates, told me that you are planning to take some trips outside the country. Is that true?"

"Yes. It is time for the whole world to see me."

"He said that you are going to Rome, India and Mecca of all places."

"And Jerusalem. I will give the religious leaders of the world the opportunity to acknowledge me." She continued eating her salad with great relish.

"The security will be quite a challenge." Perhaps Anna had lost her mind, and he briefly considered that as she looked for another croissant. If she went to the Middle East, some fanatic would certainly kill her. False prophets, especially females, are not suffered in those parts of the world.

"The leaders have assured my safety." Anna pointed to an anchovy that he had removed from his salad and placed upon his bread plate. When he nodded his affirmation, she snapped it up and popped it in her mouth.

"When will you be leaving on this journey?" His mind was moving very quickly as he could see everything come together. This woman would serve her purpose much better as a dead martyr than a live lunatic would, and her murder would be performed outside of the country by some fringe group that would be easy to demonize. Yates could then institute his big plan of creating surrogate prophets that would appear all over the globe; there could be sightings of the risen Anna Dare everywhere ministering to the poor, the ill, and the homeless. They could deposit gold coins in the Salvation Army kettle and disappear.

"Very soon. Maybe next week. The Dalai Lama and I are pen pals."

"I see." Peterson would support her now, even offer some ineffectual security for her last trip. When she left the restaurant, Anna would be pleased with herself thinking that she had charmed him, maybe believing that she was indispensable now. Her pride would be her undoing. She could not bring herself to realize that she was just a tool in his hands, that he was far superior to her.

"No, Ray of Sunshine. You do not see any of it yet, but I do. I have the voice of God in my head that tells me that all of this will be for the best, even if I am killed in the most hideous way, maybe especially if I am killed in the most hideous way." Her voice was a bit louder than he would have liked, and he noticed a few stares. He needed to calm her down.

"Anna, take a breath." She ignored him as she finished the remainder of her salad in one huge bite.

"This is the best Caesar I have ever had." She took a drink of water and shot him that deep look. "And just so you know, I don't think that you are superior to me in any way that matters."

ACKNOWLEDGEMENTS

I would like to thank the generous readers who reviewed the early versions of this book providing me feedback and much encouragement: Marianne McGee, Donna House, Christine Wallington Meyer, Dave Wallington, Jeaneen Wallington, Christine Blau, Lisa Terbrock, Steve McIntyre, Shannon O'Dougherty, and Tom House. I would have been lost without you.